THE GUNSMITH

468

Murder in the Family

Books by J.R. Roberts
(Robert J. Randisi)

The Gunsmith series

Gunsmith Giant series

Lady Gunsmith series

Angel Eyes series

Tracker series

Mountain Jack Pike series

COMING SOON!
The Gunsmith
469 – The Tall Texan

For more information visit:
www.SpeakingVolumes.us

THE GUNSMITH

468

Murder in the Family

J.R. Roberts

SPEAKING VOLUMES, LLC
NAPLES, FLORIDA
2021

Murder in the Family

ISBN 978-1-64540-433-0

Chapter One

It had been some time since Rick Hartman had sold his saloon and gambling hall, Rick's Place, and left Labyrinth, Texas. He was still trying to figure out where he would settle and start again.

He was lying in bed in his hotel room, staring at the ceiling, aware of the steady, rhythmic breathing of the woman lying next to him. Two weeks in Mission City, Texas seemed enough to almost convince him it was the place. There was a saloon for sale that he knew he could turn into another Rick's Place. All he had to do was make the right offer to the owner.

He was itching to get back into business, but he had not allowed that itch to rush him into a bad decision. He had been waiting for an opportunity like this one. And meeting Cora, the woman lying naked beside him, had been a bonus. He was going to need a woman to hire the girls for the new Rick's Place, and Cora had the experience and the taste he required.

"What are you thinking about?" Cora asked, coming awake.

"Whether or not I should call my new business Rick's Place or use a different name."

"Like what? Rick's Saloon?"

"So I like havin' my name over the door," he said, laughing.

She reached over and ran her hand across his chest.

"You should get some sleep," she said. "You can make your decisions tomorrow."

He took her hand in his and looked at her.

"Most of the big decisions I've made in my life have been at night, in bed."

"Well, then," she said, freeing her hand and sliding it down over his belly, "you've been in bed with the wrong women."

She stroked his semi-hard cock, and he responded. Then she lowered her lovely face and began to use her tongue and mouth, and he stopped thinking about his business . . .

***

Rick awoke before Cora in the morning and knew he better get up before she opened her eyes. The woman was insatiable. He slid out of bed and quietly got dressed. He wanted to get over to the Red Steer Saloon and make his offer before anybody beat him to it.

He left the room, closing the door behind him quietly, and went downstairs. He considered stopping in the hotel dining room for breakfast but decided to do it afterward.

When he reached the Red Steer, he went around to the side where there were stairs leading up to a second. He climbed the stairs and knocked on the door. He had to knock a second time before it was opened by a bleary-eyed man.

"Jesus, Hartman, what's so important you gotta see me this early? It's only six."

"I'm sorry, Mr. Lewis, but I wanted to give you my offer as soon as possible."

That woke the older man up.

"So you're ready?"

"I think I'm ready."

"Well, come on in, then," Lewis said. "I'll put on some coffee."

"Sounds good."

***

Caleb Lewis had owned the Red Steer for over twenty years, but now he was ready to get out of the saloon business. No one had offered him anywhere near his price. When Rick Hartman came to town, Lewis knew who he was. He had heard of Rick's Place in Labyrinth, Texas and knew that Hartman had sold it looking to start again. They had been talking all week coming closer and closer to a price they could both live with. Now Rick Hartman was ready to make his final offer.

They sat at a table with coffee cups, pencil and paper, scribbling numbers down for each other. Finally, Rick slid the paper over to Lewis, who read it and held out his hand.

"I think we have a deal," he said.

"Yes!" Rick said, pumping the man's hand.

"When do you want to take it over?" Lewis asked.

"As soon as we can draw up the papers, and I hand you the money," Rick said.

"That suits me," Lewis said. "I'll talk to my lawyer this morning."

"He's in town?"

Lewis nodded.

"He has an office here," Lewis said. "Come back later this afternoon, and I should have the papers."

"And I'll have a bank draft," Rick said.

The two men shook hands at the door, and Rick left, heading for the bank.

Chapter Two

Rick sat at his private table in the back of his new place, Rick's Palace. It had been open a month, and he already knew he had a success on his hands. He looked up at the crystal chandeliers hanging from the ceiling, and when he brought his eyes down, saw Cora walking toward him. She was wearing a low-cut, beautiful, beaded red gown. He stood up as she reached him and held a chair out for her.

"How is everything?" he asked, sitting across from her.

"The girls are fine," Cora said. "After a month they've got their jobs down pat."

At that moment, a pretty young blonde came over and set a glass of champagne down in front of Cora.

"Thanks, Melanie."

"Yes, Ma'am. Can I get you something, Mr. Hartman?"

"No thanks, Melanie."

"You just let me know when you want anything," Melanie said. "*Anything.*"

She flounced away.

"She likes you," Cora said. "All of the girls like you. They're . . . impressed."

"They're young," Rick said. "Too young. That's why I have you to look after them."

"I know."

He started to say something else but stopped when he saw a man approaching.

"Sheriff Erickson," he said, when the man reached them.

"Can we talk?" Erickson asked.

"This is Cora," Rick said.

"Ma'am." Erickson removed his hat.

"Sheriff," Cora stood, picked up her champagne glass and walked away.

"Have a seat, Sheriff."

Erickson sat down.

"You know why I'm here, Hartman," the lawman said.

"Tell them I said no," Rick said.

"That ain't smart," Erickson said. "Didn't Lewis tell you about this when he sold you the place?"

"No, he didn't."

"Look," Erickson said. "I don't like this any more than you do." The lawman was in his fifties, had been the law in Mission City for over twelve years. "But these are the people you have to deal with if you want to live and work in this town."

"Look," Rick said, "you set up a meetin' between me and whoever these people are, and I'll talk to them."

"That ain't the way it works," Erickson said.

"Well, that's the way it's gonna have to work if they wanna deal with me. You tell 'em that."

Erickson started to get up.

"But why don't you have a beer first?" Rick suggested. "On the house, of course." He waved at Melanie, who came running over.

"Yes, sir?"

"Bring the sheriff a beer, will you, honey?"

"Yes, sir."

She hurried off.

"Thanks, Hartman," Erickson said, settling back in his chair. "You really turned this place into somethin' special."

"That was my intention."

"I never thought Lewis would sell this place, but seein' this, I'm glad he did."

"So am I," Rick said. "I've been lookin' for somethin' just this size."

Melanie came rushing back with the sheriff's beer.

"Thank you, Ma'am," Erickson said.

"Enjoy your beer, Sheriff," Rick said, getting to his feet. "I've got to make my rounds. Make sure my customers are happy."

"They aren't the only ones you have to keep happy," Erickson said.

***

He made one full circuit of the place, greeting customers, and then stopped at the bar. Cora came walking over.

"What'd the sheriff want?"

"He wants me to meet some friends of his."

"Friends? Like who?"

"I don't know," he said, "but I told him to set it up."

"For when?"

"He'll let me know."

"You will be careful, won't you?" she asked.

"Of course," he said. "I'm always careful."

***

Three men stared at Sheriff Erickson.

"Did you explain the situation to him?" the first one asked.

"I did."

"And he said?" the second man asked.

"To tell you he wants to meet with you."

The three men exchanged a glance. They were seated at a table, with Sheriff Erickson standing in front of them.

"Did you tell him that's not the way it works?" the third man asked.

"I did."

"And?" the first man asked.

"He didn't care."

The three men exchanged a glance again.

"What do you want me to tell 'im?" Erickson asked.

"Tell him," the first man said, "that we'll meet with him."

"When?"

"Go and see him in the morning," the second man said, "and tell him we'll see him the next day, Friday."

"Where?"

"Noon, at City Hall."

"Okay."

"Tell him you'll meet him out front and bring him in," the first man said.

"Yessir."

"That's all," the first man said.

"Yes, sir."

Erickson turned and left.

After the door closed, the first man said, "I think it's time."

"Already?" the second man asked.

"Why wait?" the first man asked. "We know who he is. We can't wait until he gets stronger. He could ruin everything."

He looked at the second and third man until each of them nodded their heads.

Chapter Three

Two months later . . .

Clint Adams rode into Mission City, Texas, knowing he should have been there weeks ago. When he got the message from Rick Hartman that his new place was open, he was involved in something that took weeks to clear up. Now he was finally riding in, and as he did, he saw the large red sign over the door that read RICK'S PALACE. His friend had finally done it.

He rode his Tobiano, Toby, to the front of the saloon and dismounted. Once he tied him off, he mounted the boardwalk and entered the saloon. The chandeliers screamed his friend's handiwork.

The place was almost empty at this early time of the day. Clint approached the bar, and the bartender came over.

"Help ya?"

"Beer."

The roundly built, fiftyish bartender nodded and got him a beer.

"You can help me with something else." Clint said.

"Oh yeah? What's that?" the man leaned on the bar.

"I'm looking for Rick Hartman," Clint said. "Is he around?"

The barman straightened up, looked uncomfortable.

"Who're you?" he asked.

"Clint Adams. I'm a friend of his. I was supposed to be here weeks ago, but something came up. Can you tell me where he is?"

"Uh," the bartender said, "I think maybe you oughtta talk to Cora."

"Cora? Who's Cora?"

"Cora Nevins," the bartender said. "She . . . she's in charge of the girls here."

"And she's close to Rick?" Clint asked, with a smile. "That figures. Where is she, upstairs?"

"You stay here," the man said. "I'll get Cora to come down. She'll tell you."

"Tell me what?"

"She'll . . . tell you where Rick is."

"Look—"

The bartender hurried from behind the bar over to the stairs and trotted up. Clint sipped his beer and gave the place the once over while he waited. His friend was all over it. Not just the chandeliers, but the mahogany bar, the huge, gold-edged mirror. It was all Rick.

12

When the bartender reappeared, coming down the steps, he was followed by an attractive woman in her thirties.

"Mr. Adams," he said, coming back around the bar, "this is Cora. Cora, this is Clint Adams. He's looking for Rick."

"Otto," she said, "bring two beers back to Rick's table." Mr. Adams? Would you come with me?"

"Sure," Clint said.

He followed her to the back of the large room, to a table for two. Otto followed, put the beers down in front of them.

"Thank you, Otto," she said.

He went back to the bar.

"Mr. Adams," Cora said, "Rick has told me a lot about you."

"I haven't heard a thing about you," Clint said, "but then I've only gotten a couple of telegrams from him. One when he bought this place, and then one when he said he had it up and running."

"He was excited that day," she said. "He ran to the telegraph office to send word to you."

"I could read it in the message," Clint said. "So tell me, where is he? Still asleep? I could go up and wake his lazy ass up."

"He's not asleep, Mr. Adams," she said.

"Just call me Clint."

"Clint," she said, "he's not asleep. I'm sorry, but. . . Rick's dead."

Chapter Four

"What the hell are you talking about?" he demanded. "Dead how? When?"

"Almost two months ago," she said. "He was shot."

"Where?"

"Just outside, in the street."

"No," Clint said, closing his eyes, "I mean . . . where was he shot?"

"Oh," she said. "In the back."

"Damn it!" he hissed. Then he looked straight at her. "This can't be true."

"I'm sorry," she said, a tear rolling down her face, "but it is."

"Where is he?" he asked. "Where's his body? I want to see it."

"You can't" she said. "He was buried on Boot Hill."

Clint picked up his beer and drank half of it down, but he had to stop because he couldn't breathe.

"Damn it," he said. "I should've gotten here sooner."

She reached across the table to cover his hand with hers.

"I don't think you could've got here in time."

He slid his hand away from hers and sat back.

"Who did it? Who killed him?"

"We don't know," she said.

"We?"

"Nobody knows, Clint."

"What about the sheriff?"

"His name's Erickson," she said. "He asked around, but he didn't find any witnesses."

"What time did it happen?"

"About noon," she said. "Rick had just left the saloon. I heard the shots, came running down, but he was lying in the street."

"Shots?"

"What?"

"You said you heard the shots," he said. "How many times was he shot?"

"Twice, I think."

"Is Sheriff Erickson still working on it?"

"I assume so."

"You don't know?"

"He doesn't check in with me," she said.

He stood up.

"Where are you going?" she asked.

"To talk to the sheriff. Where's his office. I didn't see it when I rode in."

"If you stopped here, then you didn't ride far enough. It's about two more streets."

He started away, then stopped and turned back.

"What about this place?" Clint asked. "If Rick's dead, why is it still open?"

"He left a will. It said he wanted the place to stay open until the new owner arrived to make some decisions."

"And who's the new owner?" he asked. "You?"

"Me?" she asked. "No, I'm just . . . running it."

He turned and faced her.

"So who's the new owner?"

"Well . . . you are."

"What?"

"He left the place to you, Clint."

Clint stared at her, then said, "I can't deal with this now." He turned and left.

***

He took the Tobiano with him as he walked down to the sheriff's office. As he entered the office, a man looked up from the desk in the center of the room. There was a gun rack behind him, and then left a door that presumably led to a cell block.

"Are you Sheriff Erickson?" he asked.

The man was in his fifties, grey-haired, with a square chin. He nodded.

"I'm Erickson. Who're you?"

"My name's Clint Adams."

The lawman recognized the name immediately.

"What's the Gunsmith doin' in Mission City?" he asked.

"I came here to visit a friend."

"Oh," the sheriff said. "And who would that friend be?"

"His name is Rick Hartman," Clint said. "I understand you know him. Or should I say, knew him."

"I did," Erickson said. "I assume you heard. I was real sorry about his death."

"Yeah," Clint said. "Yeah, I bet you were. Do you want to tell me what you're doing about it?"

"Not much I can do," Erickson said. "I asked around, but there were no witnesses."

"At noon? In the street?"

"It was noon, and there were a lot of people on the street. Any one of them could've shot him in the back and then faded into the crowd."

"Just faded."

"That's right," Erickson said. "Gone."

"So what are you doing to find him?"

"I got the word out, but that's about all I can do."

"Well," Clint said, "I can do a lot more."

Chapter Five

As Clint left the sheriff's office, the lawman came running out after him.

"Adams!" he yelled. "What do you plan on doing?"

"What you should've done, Sheriff," he said. "Find a killer."

"And how do you plan to do that?"

"I don't know," Clint said. "I'll get my horse into a livery, and then get myself settled."

"How long would you be stayin'?"

"Until I find out who killed Rick," Clint said. "I'm not leaving until after that."

"That could be a long time," the sheriff said.

"Then I'll be here a long time," Clint said.

"Where can I find you?" Erickson called out, as he started to walk away.

"Oh, you'll find me at Rick's Palace," Clint replied. "You see, I'm the new owner."

Oh Christ, the lawman thought as Clint Adams walked away. He had to tell the others as soon as possible.

***

As anxious as Clint was to start looking into the shooting of Rick Hartman, he took the time to get his Tobiano boarded at one of the livery stables. That done, he went back to Rick's Palace, which had started to accumulate customers.

"Where's Cora?" Clint asked Otto, the bartender.

"She's upstairs, Mr. Adams," the man said. "She said to send you right up."

"Did she tell you who owns this place now?"

"She did, sir. Is there, uh, anythin' you want me to do for you?"

"For now, Otto," Clint said, "just keep doing what you've been doing."

"Yessir."

"What room is Cora's?"

"First one at the top of the stairs."

Clint crossed the saloon floor and went up the stairs. At the top he knocked on Cora's door, and she answered.

"Do you want to come in," she asked, "or see Rick's room?"

"Let me see his room," he said.

She stepped out into the hall and led him to another door.

"I suppose this'll be your room, now," she said, putting a key into the lock.

"No," Clint said, "I'll take another room if you have it, or I'll go to a hotel."

"There's a room at the end of the hall you can have," she said, pointing.

"Fine, I'll take that."

She opened the door, but didn't go in.

"I'll leave you alone," she said. "I'll be in my room if you need me. Your room will be the last one; here's the key." She took a key off the ring she was holding and handed it to him.

"Thanks." He still had his saddlebags over his shoulder and his rifle in hand. As he stepped into Rick's room and closed the door, he set the saddlebags aside.

The room was neat and clean. He didn't know if Rick kept it that way, or if it had been cleaned after his death. He shook his head. He still couldn't accept that his friend was gone. He was afraid there was only one way he would accept it, but that would come later.

He went through the drawers of a bureau, found the expensive shirts his friend had a yen for. The bed was large and had been made, there was an overstuffed chair with a small table and lamp next to it. On the table was a volume of Mark Twain's tales, which Clint didn't know his friend had developed a taste for.

He looked in the closet, found his friends jackets and not much else. A look under the bed revealed nothing. There was a small desk in a corner, but it yielded nothing, as well. Clint was sure there was an office downstairs, and that's where he had to go next. But first he decided to drop his saddlebags and rifle in "his" room.

He left Rick's room, walked to the end of the hall and unlocked the door. When he entered, he found the room as large as Rick's but not furnished as well. It had a bed, a chest of drawers, and a wooden chair in a corner. That was enough for him. He put the saddlebags on the chair and leaned the rifle against the wall. Then he left and went down the hall, back to Cora's door.

"I'm assuming Rick had an office downstairs?"

"Yes," she said, "I can come down and show you, or you could just ask Otto."

"I'll ask Otto."

"I'll be getting dressed to come down later and start work," she said. "Unless you want to fire me."

"Not at the moment," he said, "but we'll see."

She closed her door, and he went down the stairs and walked to the bar.

Chapter Six

Otto walked Clint to a door in a corner of the rear wall.

"This is the office," he said.

"Is it locked?"

"Usually," Otto said, "but not since Rick—not in a while."

"Did anyone go in after Rick was killed?"

"I know Cora's been in there," Otto said. "And the sheriff. That's about it."

"Okay, thanks. You can go back to the bar."

Otto turned and walked away as Clint opened the door and stepped inside.

The office was larger than the one Rick had in Rick's Place in Labyrinth. The desk was mahogany, large and neat. Behind the desk was a file cabinet and an expensive leather chair. Across from the desk was a leather visitor's chair, not as expensive as Rick's chair, but it still had to cost a pretty penny.

He walked around the desk and sat in his friend's chair. He remained there for a while, just sitting and seething. Rick Hartman had been his friend for a long time. Losing him was painful but hearing that he had been shot in the back was even worse. This was the second friend he had lost in that fashion, after Wild Bill Hickok.

He went through the desk drawers, didn't find much since the business had only been open a short time. Off to his right, on a sideboard, he found a bottle of the brandy his friend liked. In the bottom drawer of the desk, was a bottle of whiskey.

There was nothing in the room to indicate who might have shot him. Clint knew he was going to have to start looking into his friend's life in Mission City. In two months he had managed to buy himself a new place and get it up and running. What Clint needed to know was, had Rick made any friends during that time, and had he made any enemies?

He was going to have a longer talk with both Cora and Otto, separately, and maybe together. He would also have to find out who the other employees in the saloon were. But before any of that, he opened the bottle of his friend's whiskey and had a drink to his memory, even though he had still not accepted that he was dead.

He left the office and walked to the bar, where Otto was serving several customers. Clint waited until the man was available and waved him over.

"A drink, Mr. Adams?" Otto asked.

"No, Otto," Clint said, "I want you to tell me where the undertaker's office is."

"The undertaker?"

"I'm sure he's the one who buried Rick?"

"Oh, yeah, I see," Otto said. "Well, he's down the street about three blocks, on the left side. His name's Paul Tate, he's got a sign outside says Paul Tate, Undertaker. You ain't gonna be able to miss it."

"Thanks. Before I go, how many other people work here besides you and Cora?"

"We got three girls and one relief bartender," Otto said.

"Nobody riding shotgun?" Clint asked.

"I got a shotgun behind the bar," Otto said. "Rick always thought that was enough."

"You called him Rick?" Clint asked.

"Yes, sir," Otto said. "He insisted on that."

"Okay, then," Clint said, "you might as well call me Clint. Stop with the 'yessirs.'"

"Yess—uh, all right, Clint."

"I'm going to want to have a long talk with you later, Otto."

"Are you gonna try to find out who shot Rick?" Otto asked.

"I am going to find out who shot him, Otto," Clint said, "and I'm going to make them pay."

"Then I'll tell you everythin' I know, whenever you're ready."

"Thanks, Otto. I'll be back in a little while, if Cora's looking for me."

"I'll tell 'er."

Clint nodded and left the saloon.

***

He walked down the street and saw that Otto was right. The sign over the door was huge: PAUL TATE, UNDERTAKER. He also noticed that the undertaker's office was right across the street from the sheriff's office. He remembered seeing the big sign as he came out of the lawman's office, but it just didn't register then.

He went to the front door, found it unlocked, and entered.

***

When Cora came downstairs, she walked right to the bar and crooked her finger at Otto.

"Is Mr. Adams in the office?"

"No," Otto said. "He was, but he went over to the undertakers. And he told me to call him Clint."

"Uh-huh," she said. "Well you and me, Otto, we're going to have to get our stories straight for Clint."

"He did say he wanted to talk to me later," Otto told her.

"I'm sure he'll want to talk to both of us," Cora said. "Here's what I think . . ."

Chapter Seven

As Clint entered the office, a bell tinkled over his head and a tall, thin man came from a back room through a curtained doorway.

"Can I help you, sir?"

The man looked like the cliché of an undertaker— tall, painfully thin, very pale, with an angular face. He could've been forty or sixty.

"You can tell me if you're Paul Tate."

"I am. Are you bereaved?"

"I am, but apparently you've already buried my friend."

"Have I?"

"Yes," Clint said. "Rick Hartman?"

"Oh my," Tate said. "That was a tragedy."

"Yes," Clint said, "being shot in the back is a tragedy."

"Well, I can show you where he is buried, if you like," Tate said.

"I want a little more than that, Mr. Tate."

"Oh? And what would that be?"

"I want to see the body."

Tate stared at him for a moment before speaking.

"I'm, sorry," he said. "Did you say you want to see the body?"

"That's what I said," Clint replied. "You see, I need to make sure he's really dead before I cause a fuss."

"A fuss."

"Yes," Clint said. "If my friend is dead, I'm going to find out who did it, and then you'll have another body to bury."

"Oh my," Tate said, swallowing audibly, "you intend to kill them?"

"Yes, indeed," Clint said, "but before I do that, I have to make sure my friend is truly dead."

"And how would you want to do that, sir?"

"Easy," Clint said. "I want you to dig him up and let me take a look."

"Dig him . . . up?" Tate repeated. "I don't think that's possible—"

"Oh," Clint said, "you're going to make it possible. All we need is a shovel."

"B-but . . . I don't do the actual digging."

"Well," Clint said, "get whoever does the digging and let's go."

"N-now?"

"Right now."

"Um, my gravedigger is in the back—"

"Get him!"

Tate walked to the doorway, moved the curtain aside and called out, "Hector! Grab a shovel."

He backed away and a big man with sloping shoulders came in carrying a shovel. His face was covered with heavy black stubble.

"What're we doin'?" he asked.

"This man wants us to dig a grave," Tate said.

"Well, that's my job. Where's the body?" Hector asked.

"It's already in the ground," Tate said. "This man wants us to dig it up."

"What?"

"It's simple," Clint said. "I want a look inside Rick Hartman's coffin."

"What fer?"

"Because before I kill someone for shooting him, I have to make sure he's really dead."

"And who are you?" Hector asked.

"My name's Clint Adams."

Hector's eyes went wide, and he said, "Clint Adams?"

"That's right."

"Oh, my," Tate said.

"Let's go," Clint said.

***

30

When they got to Boot Hill Clint said to Hector, "Okay, where is it?"

"Over here." Hector led Clint to the grave, which had a cross on it as a marker, but nothing with Rick's name.

"Okay, dig it up," Clint said.

"I dunno . . . is this legal?" Hector asked. "Don't we need the sheriff?"

"You don't need the sheriff," Clint said. "All you need is me. Dig."

Hector looked at Tate.

"Better do like he says, Hector."

Hector started digging.

It took a while to get six feet down, but Hector's shovel finally struck something. He cleared the dirt away, and they were looking at the lid of a coffin.

"That's a cheap box," Clint said.

"Well," Tate said, "the town paid for it."

"Get the lid off."

Hector used the edge of the shovel to pry the lid up on one side, then got his fingers underneath it and heaved it open.

There, lying on his back with his arms crossed, was the body of Rick Hartman.

Chapter Eight

"Cover him up!" Clint snapped.

Hector put the lid back on.

"You want me to bury him again?" he asked.

Clint's mind was reeling. At that moment he wanted to shoot someone—anyone. He glared at both Tate and Hector and waited for the feeling to pass.

"No," he said. "No, I'm going to pay for a better coffin and a headstone."

That seemed to brighten Paul Tate's mood.

"Well," he said, "we can go back to my place right now, and I can show you—"

"Not yet," Clint said. "First I've got to find the man who shot him."

Tate and Hector exchanged a glance.

"If either one of you know anything, you better tell me now," he said.

"We don't know anythin', Mr. Adams," Tate said. "We just buried your friend."

"Go on back to your place, then," Clint said. "I'll see you when I have another body for you to plant."

"Yessir!" Tate said.

Hector climbed up out of the hole, and the two men walked back to town.

***

"Where is he?" the first man asked Sheriff Erickson.

"I don't know where he went after he left my office," Erickson said.

"You should've put him in a cell," the second man said.

"On what charge?"

"Never mind that. What else did he tell you?"

"Just that he's gonna do somethin' about his friend bein' shot."

"All right, Sheriff," the first man said, "just keep an eye on him."

"Yessir." The sheriff left the room.

"That's all we need is the Gunsmith in town," the third man said. "We need to get him out."

"Erickson can't do the job," the first man said.

"Then we need to find somebody who can," the second man said.

"Or," the first man said, "we need to give Adams what he wants."

"What are we going to give him?" the second man asked.

The first man looked at him and said, "A shooter."

***

Clint went back to Rick's Palace, which was starting to fill up. Cora happened to be standing at the bar, talking to Otto. He joined them.

"When do the gaming tables open?" he asked.

"Pretty soon," she said. "But I thought—"

"Open them," Clint ordered. "Just run this place like normal, for now. When do the girls come down?"

"Usually, they'd be down here already."

"Well, go and get them," Clint said. "I want everyone to think everything's fine."

"Are you, uh, satisfied that Rick is really dead?" she asked.

"I saw his body," he said. "That doesn't mean I'm satisfied. Not by a long shot."

"You saw him? You mean . . . you dug him up?"

"I had the undertaker do it," Clint said. "And I'm going to buy him a better coffin, when I'm done."

"And when will you be done?" Otto asked.

"After I've killed the man who killed Rick," Clint said. "And, if need be, whoever sent him to do it."

"You'll kill two men, just like that?" Cora asked.

"At least two," he replied, "just like that." He turned to Otto. "Let's talk back at Rick's table. If you don't mind, Cora."

"I'll cover the bar til you get back," Cora told Otto.

Clint and Otto walked to the back table attracting some attention from the customers who wondered who Clint was.

"Otto, tell me about Rick's life here."

"Not much to tell," Otto said, "mainly 'cause I don't know much. I worked for Rick, but we didn't see each other outside of the saloon."

"Do you know if he made any friends while he was here?" Clint asked.

"Not that I know of," Otto said. "He was pretty busy, first buying this place, then renovating it, and finally openin' it."

"Then I suppose you can't tell me if he had any enemies."

"Don't know how he could have made enemies durin' the short time he lived here."

"No friends, no enemies," Clint said. "And women?"

"Cora was his woman, as far as I know," Otto said.

"How did they meet?"

"Cora was working in one of the other saloons in town," Otto said.

"She didn't have another man, did she? Before him? Maybe one who got jealous?"

"Cora didn't have much use for the men in this town," Otto said. "That's probably why she liked Rick."

"Okay, Otto," Clint said, "you can go back to work. Ask Cora to come back here, will you?"

"Sure thing, Clint."

Otto rose and walked to the bar.

Chapter Nine

Cora came over to the table carrying a beer for Clint and a glass of champagne for herself.

"A little early for champagne, isn't it?" he asked, as she sat.

"I've been drinking more and earlier since Rick was killed," Cora said.

"You were his woman, weren't you?"

"As much as any woman could be," she said. "I knew it wouldn't last, but it was fine for a while."

Clint knew what she meant. Rick went from woman to woman and didn't stay with one very long.

"But it was still going on when he was killed, right?" he asked.

"Yes, it was."

"Then you were privy to some pillow talk that nobody else was," he said. "Who were his friends in town? And who were his enemies?"

"I don't think he was here long enough to acquire either," she said. "He was friendly with some men who came here to drink, but the only real friend he ever spoke of was you."

"And enemies?"

"Well . . . the other saloon owners are competition," she said. "Would that make them enemies?"

"It might," Clint said. "I'm going to have to talk to them. Who are they?"

"Rance Edwards owns the Blue Slipper Saloon," she said, "and Charles Bennett owns the Bent Tree Saloon. Folks call him Charlie."

"Now tell me who runs the town?" he said.

"Well, there's Mayor Pierpont, and the members of the Town Council—"

"No," Clint said, "I mean who owns the town? If Rick decided to settle here, it had to be because he saw potential for growth."

"That's true," she said. "Mission City is on the upswing."

"Then somebody's in it to make money," Clint said. "Tell me who that is. Who owns most of the town?"

"You're talking about Dan Reed," she said. "He's got a big ranch outside of town and owns quite a few businesses."

"That's who I want," he said. "He's a man who would be trying to buy even more businesses, especially one he thought had the potential to grow."

"You think he was trying to buy Rick out?"

"I don't know," Clint said. "Was anybody making offers?"

"We had just opened, Clint," she said. "Wouldn't that happen later?"

"If somebody knew Rick's reputation, they'd be trying to buy in right away," Clint said. "Maybe not buy him out but get a piece. And if I know Rick, he wasn't about to sell a piece to anyone. In that way, he made enemies. He didn't like anybody trying to share in his success."

"Well, you could be talking about Reed," Cora said, "or there could be others."

"I'll want you to make me a list of names," Clint said. "Anybody you think is a major player in town."

"You'll take my word for that?"

"You were Rick's woman," he said. "That means he saw everything you have to offer. You're beautiful, I can see that, but he saw your intelligence, as well. So yes, I'll take your word for it."

For a moment she blushed, then took hold of herself and drank some champagne.

"I'll make that list for you," she said, "but I don't want to be the reason you kill someone."

"I'm only going to kill whoever killed Rick or had him killed. And it'll be their fault, not yours."

"All right," she said. "I'll have that list for you by tonight. But right now, I better go and get my girls ready."

"Thanks, Cora."

She reached across the table and took his hand.

"Clint, I'm so very sorry about Rick," she said. "I know you and he were very close. He thought the world of you."

"I'll never forgive myself for not getting here sooner," Clint said. "But I'm here now, and whoever killed him is going to pay."

She drew her hand back because the look of hatred in his eyes frightened her.

"See you tonight," she said, stood and headed for the stairs.

Clint picked up his beer and drank it down. He wanted a whiskey, but he remembered how the death of Wild Bill Hickok—his closest friend at that time—had driven him right into a bottle. He was lucky he was able to crawl back out, but he wasn't sure he'd be able to do it again. Losing two friends to backshooters was almost too much to take.

He decided to just have another beer and carried his empty mug to the bar.

Chapter Ten

Clint watched as three girls came down the stairs, with Cora right behind them. They were all in their twenties, one blonde, one brunette and one redhead. Leave it to Rick to hire a variety.

Cora brought the girls right over to Clint.

"Girls, this is the new owner," she said, "Clint Adams. Clint, Melanie, Abby and Angela."

Melanie, the blonde, had very clear blue eyes and the palest skin. The brunette, Abby, had the prettiest face. Angela, the redhead, had the prerequisite freckles across the bridge of her nose and in the cleft between her generous breasts.

"Ladies, it's my pleasure," Clint greeted them.

"The pleasure is all ours, Mr. Adams," Melanie said.

"We're so sorry about what happened to Mr. Hartman," Abby said.

"It was horrible," Angela said. "He was such a nice man."

"Thank you, ladies."

"And now, girls," Cora said, "off to work."

The three of them moved to start working the room, taking drink orders and putting smiles on the faces of the customers.

"We'll get the gaming tables going, too," Cora said. "Otto?"

"Yes, Ma'am."

"Otto," Clint said, "as new owner I'm naming Cora manager of the saloon. She gives the orders."

Otto smiled. "It's been that way for a while, Clint."

"Well," Clint said, "now it's official."

As Otto moved away Cora asked, "Why am I giving the orders, and not you?"

"Because I won't be around here that much," Clint said. "Not while I'm looking for Rick's killer."

"Well," she said, "I'll keep everything running smoothly until you *are* around here."

"I know you will. I trust you."

"Why would you trust me so soon?" she asked. "We've only just met."

"Because Rick trusted you," Clint said.

"I'll try to deserve it," she promised.

"See you later, Cora."

Clint headed for the door. He had a couple of other saloons to visit.

***

When he reached the Blue Slipper, he stopped outside to stare at the sign over the door. Somebody had painted a blue slipper, with the word "Blue" above it and "Slipper" below.

He went inside and found the place already getting busy, although it was early evening. It didn't seem to Clint he had only ridden in that morning, so much had already happened.

Looking around he saw a couple of girls working the floor, some private poker games going on, but no house games. Behind the bar, a tall, dark-haired man in his fifties was tending. Clint walked over.

The bartender, chewing on a toothpick, asked, "What can I get ya?"

"A beer."

"Comin' up."

When he brought the beer over Clint asked, "Is the owner around? Mr. Edwards, isn't it?"

"That's right, Rance Edwards," the bartender said. "Who wants 'im?"

"Tell him the new owner of Rick's Palace."

The bartender frowned.

"Too bad about what happened to that feller," he said. "He seemed a decent sort."

"It's going to be too bad for whoever killed him when I find him," Clint said.

43

"I'll, uh, see if Mr. Edwards is around."

"Much obliged," Clint said.

He sipped his beer and watched the activity in the saloon, all of which had become traditional—drinking, laughing, gambling, grabbing for the girls. This is what you expected to see in a saloon. And then, as it got later and the men got more liquored up, there'd be the inevitable fights, which could become anything from laughable to deadly.

When the bartender returned, there was a man walking behind him, wearing a grey suit and tie. He was in his forties, with very well-groomed hair and mustache.

"I hear you're the new owner of Rick's Palace," he said, immediately. "I'm Rance Edwards."

"Mr. Edwards." They shook hands. "My name is Clint Adams."

Edwards withdrew his hand very slowly.

"Did you say Adams?"

"That's right."

"I heard that Hartman was friends with the Gunsmith," Edwards said. "Did his murder bring you here?"

"I'm afraid I didn't hear Rick was dead until I rode into town this morning."

"It must have come as a shock."

"A big shock," Clint said. "Do you have time to talk to me about it?"

"Well, sure," Edwards said. "I don't know how much I can tell you, but why don't you come to my office." He looked at the bartender. "Auggie, bring a couple of fresh beers to my office."

"You got it, boss."

"This way, Mr. Adams."

He started across the room, and Clint followed.

Chapter Eleven

Edwards' office was smaller than Rick's, and slightly cramped with two people in it. He sat behind a small, oak desk and invited Clint to sit across from him.

As they settled into chairs, the bartender came in with two beers, set them down and left.

"That one is on the house, by the way," he said.

"Thank you," Clint said, but left the beer sitting on the desk.

"How can I help you, Mr. Adams?"

"I'm trying to figure out if Rick had any enemies in town," Clint said.

"Enemies," Edwards said, shaking his head. "I can't say for sure, but I don't see how he could. He wasn't here long enough to form friendships or make enemies."

"So you didn't see him as competition for you and your place?"

"Oh, of course he was competition," Edwards said. "He was offering things that we don't. But that certainly wouldn't be a reason for me to kill him."

"What about the other saloon in town?"

"Charlie Bennett at the Bent Tree?" Edwards asked. "Charlie is the most affable man you'd ever want to meet. No, no, Charlie and Rick were not enemies."

"How about anyone else in town?" Clint asked. "The mayor? Or members of the Town Council?"

Edwards frowned.

"Now, I wouldn't know about that. I don't know what contact Hartman had with the politicians in town. You'll have to find that out for yourself."

"Tell me about Mayor Pierpont," Clint said. "All I've got is his name."

"He's been mayor for several years, before that was a member of the Council for some time. He's in his sixties, so I don't believe he has any ambitions beyond his present position. But he does intend to make more improvements in town."

"Does the Council usually go along with him?"

"Pretty much."

"Are you on the Council?"

Edwards smiled.

"I am not," he said. "They wouldn't want me, as I tend to have a mind of my own."

"I see."

"Now can I ask you a question?"

"Sure."

"As the new owner, what do you intend to do with the place?"

"I really haven't decided, and I can't think about that now," Clint said. "I won't be thinking about anything else until I find out who killed Rick and make them pay."

"Make them pay?"

Clint picked up his beer and said, "I'm going to kill them."

***

After Clint thanked Edwards for his time and the beer, he left then headed over to the Bent Tree to see the "affable" Charlie Bennett.

The Bent Tree was on a par with the Blue Slipper. It was about the same size and seemed to be doing the same amount of business. Clint had the feeling Rick's Palace was taking a lot of business away from these other two saloons. The owners were being very reasonable if they didn't consider him an enemy.

As he approached the bar, he saw that a woman was tending. She smiled as he approached, revealing herself to be a very pretty thirty or so. She wore a simple dress rather than the kind of gown a saloon girl would usually wear.

"Hello, stranger," she said, "What can I do for you?"

"Well," Clint said, "I'll take a beer to start with, and then I'd like to talk to the owner, Mr. Bennett."

"Nobody calls him 'Mister' Bennett," she said. "Everybody just calls him Charlie." She set a beer down in front of him.

"Well," he asked, "is Charlie available?"

"He's around here someplace, so I'd say he's available," she said. "Who's askin'?"

"My name is Clint Adams," he said. "I'm the new owner of Rick's Palace."

She lost her smile.

"Poor Mr. Hartman," she said. "That was a terrible thing."

"Yes, it was," he said. "I'd like to talk to Charlie about it."

"Do you think Charlie did it?" she asked.

"I simply want to know what Charlie knows, or has heard," Clint said, "since I've only just got to town. Rick and I were friends."

"I'm sorry for your loss, then," she said. "Let me find Charlie and tell him you're here. I'm sure he'll be willin' to talk with you."

Chapter Twelve

Charlie Bennett came out and shook hands enthusiastically with Clint. He was about five-foot five, late thirties, with lots of energy.

"It's a pleasure to meet the Gunsmith," he said, "I'm just sorry it's under these circumstances. I'm so sorry about what happened to Mr. Hartman. Listen, my office is a mess, but there's a back room here where we can talk. Ellie, would you bring two beers?"

As with Rance Edwards, Clint followed Bennett across the floor to the back room, where he found a round table and five chairs.

"Have a seat, have a seat," Bennett said.

Ellie came in right behind them and set down two beers.

"Thanks, Ellie," Bennett said.

She withdrew.

"What can I do for you, Mr. Adams?"

"I'm intent on finding out who killed Rick Hartman," Clint said.

"Well, yes, of course. He was your friend. It makes sense you'd want the killer brought to justice."

"Not to justice," Clint said. "I'm going to kill them."

Bennett looked shocked.

"That might be a problem when it comes right down to it, sir," he said. "I mean, with Sheriff Erickson—"

"I think the sheriff knows better than to get in my way," Clint said.

"Well then, I sure wouldn't want to be the one to get in your way, either. What can I do for you?"

Clint had the same conversation with Bennett that he'd had with Edwards about friends and enemies, and the result was about the same.

"It seems like you and Mr. Edwards had pretty good attitudes toward a man who was taking some of your business."

"I believe there are plenty of men in town who want drinks, Mr. Adams," Bennett said. "Certainly enough to keep three saloons busy."

"Even in a town this size?"

"This town is gonna grow," Bennett said. "The mayor's very serious about that."

"Well," Clint said, "somebody was concerned about Rick, enough to kill him."

"Like I said," Bennett replied, "I'm real sorry about that, but I don't know anythin' helpful. I wish I did, Mr. Adams. I really don't like the idea of a saloon owner getting' killed. It strikes too close to home."

"Thanks for your time," Clint said, standing.

Bennett also stood.

"If you do think of somethin' I can do to help you, please let me know," he said.

"Oh, I will," Clint said.

Bennett walked Clint out to the front doors and watched him leave. Then he turned and went to the bar.

"What was that all about?" Ellie asked.

"He's out to kill somebody," Bennett said.

"Who?"

"Whoever killed Rick Hartman."

"And he's just going to find him and kill him?"

"Yes."

"Does he expect to get away with it?"

Bennett shrugged.

"He's the Gunsmith," he said. "That's what he does, ain't it?"

"I suppose so."

"Well," Bennett said, "it's not gonna affect us or our business. I'll be in my office."

"All right, Charlie."

As Bennett walked to the back, Ellie leaned on the bar and wondered where Clint Adams was staying.

***

Clint returned to Rick's Palace, which was extremely busy. So much so that Otto and Cora were behind the bar, working it together.

It looked as if the Palace was doing more business than the Blue Slipper and Bent Tree combined. That certainly didn't support Charlie Bennett's comment that there were enough men in town to support three saloons.

Clint went to the crowded bar and managed to elbow himself a space.

"There you are," Cora said. "How'd it go?"

"Not great. I talked to Edwards and Bennett," Clint said. "I got the same story from both. They don't know anything helpful."

"So what's your next move?" she asked.

"Tomorrow I'll talk to the mayor," Clint said. "But for now, I'm going upstairs and get some sleep."

"Good," she said, "I'm sure you need it."

"I'll see you and Otto in the morning," Clint said, and headed for the stairs.

Chapter Thirteen

Clint was surprised he slept so well with all the activity going on below him. He wasn't sure what time Otto and Cora closed the saloon, but it didn't matter. He fell asleep before that anyway.

He did wake to the smell of coffee, though, and came down to find Otto behind the bar.

"Did you get any sleep?" Clint asked.

"Oh yeah, but Rick used to like to wake up to coffee, and I got into the habit. Want a cup?"

"Sure," Clint said.

Most of the chairs were on the tables, but for one. Clint sat there and Otto brought him a cup.

"What about Cora and the girls?"

"They never come down early," Otto said.

"Well, this'll be enough to get me started, but where can I go for a good breakfast?"

"Down the street. The place is called The Rainbow Café. Don't ask me why. There are no rainbows there, but the food's good."

"Are they busy?"

"Yeah, they do a breakfast rush," Otto said. "You're bound to find some shopkeepers there before they open their stores, and on occasion the mayor eats there."

"Well," Clint said, "that would be interesting, since I'm looking to meet him today."

"Your best bet for that would be to have Sheriff Erickson take you to City Hall and introduce you," Otto said. "Otherwise you might have trouble gettin' in to see him."

"Well, nobody's going to keep me from meeting him, but I'll take your advice and see the sheriff first anyway."

Clint had a second cup of coffee, thanked Otto and left the saloon to walk to the Rainbow Café.

***

Otto was right about the breakfast rush, and since most people like to sit at tables in front or even the center of the room, Clint had no trouble getting one against the back wall. From there he could see all the other diners, most of whom did look like shopkeepers, as Otto said.

He didn't see anyone who looked like the mayor, but that was okay. He preferred to eat his breakfast alone.

When the waiter came, he ordered steak-and-eggs. He figured he might as well test their cook by ordering his favorite breakfast. It came with the meat and eggs looking perfect, along with spuds and biscuits. Otto had been right again. There were no rainbows, but the food was good.

After breakfast, he walked to the sheriff's office, hoping to find him in. As he entered, he saw, with satisfaction, that the man was at his desk.

"You come to work early," he said.

"It's my job," Erickson said. "What can I do for you?"

"Easy," Clint said. "Take me to meet the mayor."

"Why?"

"I talked with the owners of the other saloons," Clint said. "They couldn't tell me a thing. So I want to talk to Mayor Pierpont."

"What's he gonna tell ya?"

"I won't know until I talk to him, will I?"

"Look, you're determined to kill whoever killed your friend. If you think it's the mayor—"

"You don't have to worry, Sheriff," Clint said, "that is, unless it was you?"

"Why would I kill Mr. Hartman?"

"I don't know," Clint said. "That's what I'm trying to find out, isn't it? You want to get in my way?"

Erickson sat back in his chair and put his hands up.

"Not me," the lawman said. "I'm not about to go up against the Gunsmith. You wanna meet the mayor? Be my guest. Let's go."

Sheriff Erickson stood, grabbed his hat and led the way out the door.

***

At City Hall Clint waited outside the mayor's office while Erickson went in.

"You did what? You brought Adams here?"

"He wants to meet you," Erickson said. "It was either bring him here or eat a bullet."

The mayor laughed.

"You think he would've killed you if you didn't bring him here?"

"I don't know what he'll do," Erickson said. "But his friend is dead, and he's got crazy eyes. So I think you better talk to him, and convince him you're not involved."

"Yes, all right, Sheriff," Mayor Pierpont said. "Bring the Gunsmith in."

Erickson went to the door, stuck his head out and said, "The Mayor will see you now."

Chapter Fourteen

Clint walked into the office and the mayor said, "That'll be all, Sheriff."

"Yes, sir."

Erickson left and closed the door.

"Mr. Adams?" the older man said. "I'm Mayor Pierpont."

"The sheriff tell you why I'm here, Mr. Mayor?" Clint asked.

"Yes," Pierpont said, sitting back in his chair. "You're in town because of Rick Hartman's murder."

"What can you tell me?"

"Me? Nothing," Pierpont said. "I heard he was shot, and that's all I know."

"People in town tell me you have big plans for Mission City."

"I do," the mayor said.

"Well, I'm sure Rick had big plans, too," Clint said. "Maybe his plans didn't match yours?"

"What are you trying to say, Mr. Adams?" the mayor asked. "That the mayor of Mission City had a man killed?"

"Are you saying that's never happened?" Clint asked. "Politicians are politicians."

"Ah, I get it," Pierpont said. "You don't like politicians."

"No, you're wrong," Clint said. "I hate politicians. I've known too many who bend the rules to get what they want."

"And you're calling murder bending the rules?" Pierpont asked.

"I'm calling this murder something I'm not going to stand for," Clint said.

"You're not the law, Adams," the mayor said. "You can't—"

"In this instance, Mr. Mayor," Clint said, "I can do whatever the hell I want. When I find out who killed my friend, I'll take care of them my way. Was it you? Did you have him killed?"

"No!" Pierpont said. He was reacting to what Sheriff Erickson had said. Clint Adams did have crazy eyes. The last thing the mayor wanted to do was die in his office. "I did not have Rick Hartman killed. I had no reason."

"Okay," Clint said. "You know everything that goes on in this town. Who do you think was responsible?"

"I have no idea," Pierpont said. "I swear. Come on, the man had only lived here for two months. How could he have made that kind of enemy?"

"I don't know," Clint said. "But I'm going to find out." After a moment he asked, "What about women? Was Rick seeing someone who might've had a boy-friend? A husband?"

"As far as I know, your friend's woman was Cora Nevins. And I never heard that she was married."

"But there could be another man, somewhere," Clint commented.

"I suppose so," the mayor said to himself.

"Mayor Pierpont," Clint said, "I need you to write down the names of the people on your Town Council, and where I can find them."

That made the mayor frown.

"Are you going to talk to each one of them?" he asked Clint.

"I am."

"I can't have you shooting my Town Council Mr. Adams," Mayor Pierpont said.

"Hey, if they had nothing to do with killing Rick Hartman, they have nothing to worry about."

The mayor hesitated, scowled, then reluctantly wrote the information down on a slip of paper and passed it across to Clint.

"Much obliged," Clint said.

"Look, Mr. Adams," Pierpont said, "nobody in this town can go against you with a gun—"

"Well, somebody's sure going to have to," Clint said, standing up, "when I find them. If you know who it is, tell them that."

"I've already told you, I don't know anything," the mayor said.

"Yes, I know you told me that, Mr. Mayor," Clint said, "but you're a politician, and we both know politicians lie, so you'll excuse me if I'm a little skeptical."

"Yes, we do lie," Pierpont admitted, "all the time, in fact, particularly during a close campaign. But I'm not lying now."

"I wish I could take your word for that, Mr. Mayor," Clint said, "I really do."

Clint turned and headed for the door.

"Mr. Adams?"

Clint turned.

"Yes?"

"Just how much proof are you going to require before you pull the trigger?"

"Undeniable proof, Mr. Mayor," Clint said. "I don't take it lightly when I kill a man."

Chapter Fifteen

When Clint left the mayor's office, he didn't find Sheriff Erickson waiting outside. He carefully exited the building, almost expecting to hear a shot, but it never came. He would have to avoid being shot in the back, himself, in order to get revenge for Rick Hartman. It would help to have someone watching his back. He could send some telegrams to friends of his, but by the time a Bat Masterson or Talbot Roper got there, it might be too late. No, he was going to have to do this himself, which was just as well. After all Rick Hartman was his friend.

There were four members of the Town Council, all of them businessmen who had their stores in town. Clint had neither met nor heard of any of them since he arrived.

As he walked away from City Hall, he got an idea. He would allow the mayor to warn each member of the Council that he was coming to see them, but then he'd wait. Their nerves would be shaken by the time he talked with them.

He returned to Rick's Palace. It was early afternoon, so there weren't many drinkers yet. Otto was behind the bar, and Cora and the other girls were nowhere in sight.

"You ready for a beer?" Otto asked.

"Coffee, if you've still got it."

"I always keep a pot goin'."

Otto got Clint a mug of coffee and set it down on the bar.

"Whataya been up to?" he asked.

Clint gave him the piece of paper the mayor had given him. Otto took it and read it.

"This is a list of the Town Council," he observed.

"Is that all of them?"

"Looks like it." Otto gave the list back. "Where'd you get it?"

"From the mayor."

"So you met Pierpont," Otto said. "What'd you think?"

"He's a politician," Clint said. "That's all I need to know."

"So's he tryin' to pin Rick's murder on one of the Council?"

"No, I asked him for the list," Clint said, putting it back in his pocket. "I'm going to talk to them."

"When?" Otto asked.

"Soon," Clint said. "I'm giving him time to let them know."

Otto laughed.

"You're makin' 'em sweat."

"That's right."

"I like it."

Clint sipped his coffee, looked around the saloon.

"When do they start coming in?" he asked.

"Any minute," Otto said. "Of course, the word is out now that you own the place."

"Is that going to cut down on business, or increase it?" Clint asked.

"That's a good question," Otto said. "We might get some extras who wanna be around when the shootin' starts, but others might stay away for that same reason."

"I guess we'll just have to wait and see."

"You meet anybody else interestin'?" Otto asked.

"When I went to the Bent Tree, there was a gal named Ellie behind the bar. Is she the regular bartender, there?"

"Pretty much," Otto said. "Bennett wanted to do somethin' different, so he tried her behind the bar. It seems to work for them."

"I suppose."

"What'd you think of those other two places?"

"I don't think they'll be much competition for Rick's," Clint said.

"Not likely," Otto said. "Rick made sure this place had everythin' they have, and a lot more."

"That was Rick's way," Clint said. "Give the customers what they want and then more."

"Do you think you'll keep it that way?" Otto asked. "I mean, I'm just curious about changes you might be wantin' to make."

"If you're worried about your job, don't be" Clint said. "I'm not about to start making big changes. I'm assuming Rick had this place running the way he wanted it."

"From what I could see, he was pretty happy with things the way they were goin'," Otto agreed.

"And maybe him being happy made others unhappy," Clint said.

"Well, you talked to Edwards and Bennett," Otto said. "What'd you think?"

"I'm not making any decisions yet," Clint said. "I've still got a lot of others to talk to, first." He pushed the empty mug away. "Thanks for the coffee."

"Where to now?"

"I think I'll head over to the undertaker's and pick Rick's headstone out," Clint said, "then get him a new coffin. I need to put him back in the ground and let him rest."

"Then I guess we'll see ya later," Otto said.

Clint turned and left the saloon.

Chapter Sixteen

Tate, the undertaker, immediately became nervous when Clint entered his office.

"Take it easy," Clint said. "I'm just here to choose a coffin and headstone."

"Well," Tate said, "I can show you what we have in the back."

They went to the back area, where Clint picked out a top-of-the-line coffin for his friend's body. Of course, he knew Rick Hartman wasn't there anymore, but just on the off chance he was, he wanted his friend to be comfortable.

As for the headstone, Clint had different stones to choose from. He finally made his choice, then gave Tate the inscription he wanted on it.

They returned to the front office, and Clint paid the bill with no complaints.

"I want all this done before I leave town," he said.

"And when do you think that will be, sir?" Tate asked.

"After I've killed the man who killed my friend," Clint said, and left.

***

Sheriff Erickson looked across the clearing at the clump of trees on the other side. Abruptly, a man stepped into view. He was tall, rangy, wearing a holstered gun on his left hip.

They approached each other and met in the center of the clearing.

"You sent word that you needed to see me?" the man asked.

"It's good to see you, too, Tillman."

"I didn't say it was good to see you, Sherriff." Tillman said. "What's on your mind?"

"We might have a problem."

"Who's we?"

"The town."

"That doesn't include me," Tillman said.

"Well, we might have to employ you."

"That's different," Tillman said. "Who do you want me to kill?"

"Who said we wanted you to kill anyone?"

"Erickson," Tillman said, "I'm not one of those money guns who doesn't know he's a money gun. I'm for hire, and it's never for anythin' but killin'. Now, I'll ask again, who do you want me to kill?"

Erickson hesitated, then said, "Clint Adams."

Tillman's face betrayed the surprise he felt.

"The Gunsmith?" he said. "What's he doin' in Mission City?"

"He was friends with Rick Hartman," Erickson said. "He says he's gonna find out who killed Hartman, and he's gonna kill 'im."

"A man after my own heart," Tillman said. "Says what he means."

"We can't have that, Tillman."

Tillman looked down at his boots, then up again at the lawman.

"This one will be expensive," he said.

"I figured. How much?"

"I'll come up with a number," Tillman said, "and you'll pay it."

"When?"

"I gotta think on it," Tillman said. "I might need another man or two."

"You wouldn't take him face-to-face?"

"That's what I gotta think on," Tillman said. "A man with that reputation, for that long, might've slowed down some."

"How're you gonna find that out unless you face him?" Erickson asked.

"Why don't you face 'im, Sheriff?" Tillman said.

Erickson snorted.

"I know I can't beat 'im," he said. "I have no illusions about my abilities with a gun. For me it's just a tool."

"For me it's an extension of my hand," Tillman said, sticking his hand out and staring at it.

"I'd sure like to see you and Adams in the street, Tillman," Erickson said.

"That's because you wouldn't care which one of us ends up dead, Sheriff."

Tillman kicked at the dirt on the ground a bit, while he thought.

"So what do I tell them, Tillman?" Erickson asked. "They're waitin'."

"Tell 'em I'll be in touch."

"It's got to be before Clint Adams finds his man," Erickson said.

"I won't be long," Tillman said. "You'll hear from me soon."

Tillman turned, walked back towards the trees and disappeared among them.

Erickson turned and headed back to his horse. The meeting had taken place a short distance from town, far enough away so nobody saw them, but too far for him to have walked.

He mounted his horse and headed back to town.

Chapter Seventeen

With the details of Rick Hartman's burial taken care of, Clint headed back to the Palace. As he entered, he saw that Cora and the girls had not yet come down from their rooms, but there *was* a woman standing at the far end of the bar. As he got closer, he recognized her as Ellie, the bartender from the Bent Tree.

"The lady came in lookin' for you," Otto said.

"She say why?"

"Nope."

"Okay, thanks, Otto. I'll take a beer at the end and bring her another of whatever she's drinking."

"Champagne," Otto said.

"Why am I not surprised."

He walked down to her end of the bar. When she saw him, she smiled.

"I heard you were looking for me," he said, as Otto followed with their drinks.

"I was," Ellie said, picking up her champagne. "Thank you."

They both drank.

"What's on your mind, Ellie?" he asked.

"Well," she said, "I thought maybe we could talk in private?"

"I suppose we could go back to Rick's office," Clint said. "It's probably my office, now."

"And would you have somethin' even . . . more private?"

"I have a room upstairs."

"That sounds better," she said.

"Okay, well, if you don't mind risking your reputation—" he started.

"Don't worry about my reputation," she said, cutting him off. "I'm a bartender, remember?"

"Let's go, then," Clint said. He looked over at Otto and pointed up, indicating he'd be in his room. The bartender nodded.

They walked together to the stairs, and then Clint moved behind her as they went up. He was aware that some of the patrons in the place were watching them.

They walked to the end of the hall til they reached his room, where he unlocked the door and opened it to let her go in first. He followed, and then closed the door behind them.

"So, Ellie," he asked, "what's on your mind? Is this about Rick Hartman?"

"Not really," she said. "It's more about, well, me."

"Then what can I do for you?"

"Well, you'll think me forward," she said, "but I'd like you to take off your pants."

***

Tillman usually thought better when he was causing somebody pain. There were times he preferred it to be a woman, which then combined pain and sex. Other time, he simply enjoyed beating on some man, each blow from his fist seeming to make his thoughts more clear. He didn't understand the reason for it, he only knew that it worked.

After Sheriff Erickson had asked him about killing the Gunsmith, Tillman had to give it a lot of thought. One of his usual victims was a man named Horace who knew what was going to happen whenever Tillman came looking for him.

Tillman drove his fist into Horace's face, knocking the man off his feet. Then, giving him time to regain his feet, he considered his options. He could face the Gunsmith alone, man-to-man, and see if he could outdraw him. Doing so would enhance his own reputation. But, of course, failing meant he would die.

He hit Horace again, and this time the man staggered but did not go down. Horace was a thickly built man in his thirties, and since he always needed money, he was always available to Tillman for one of his think sessions.

Tillman hit him again, this time taking him off his feet.

His second option was to face Clint Adams with some backup. If he and two or three other men managed to kill Adams, it would still enhance his reputation. But he'd need to choose the right men, men who would look at the situation the same way he did, as a chance to improve themselves at the risk of dying. That meant he'd have to be paid enough money to also pay them enough to make it worth their while.

Horace got to his feet, so Tillman stepped in, hit him in the stomach, and then again in the face. He used his right hand—his gun hand—for the stomach punch, because it would do the least damage. He hit him in the face with his left hand, because even if he bruised or broke a finger or two on the left, it would not affect his gunplay.

Tillman stepped back and looked down at the fallen man. With blood leaking from the corner of his mouth, and a gash on his cheek, Horace stood up.

"Okay, Horace," Tillman said, holding some money out to the man, "thanks."

"You figure it out, Mr. Tillman?" Horace asked, accepting the money.

"I have, thanks."

Horace saluted Tillman with the money and said, "Any time, Mr. Tillman."

As they left the alley, Tillman was thinking about the two men he'd choose to watch his back.

Chapter Eighteen

"My pants?" Clint asked.

"Well," Ellie said, "naturally your gunbelt first, but then yes, your pants, and everything else. You see, when you walked into the Bent Tree, I knew you were the one."

"The one . . . what?" he asked.

"The one for me," she said. "The man I could have sex with, and nobody would care."

"Why would anybody care who you have sex with?" he asked.

"Look, I'm a bartender; I deal with men every day," she said. "They get flirtatious, they get handsy, but they know they hafta stop at a certain point. But nobody's gonna blink at this."

"You think nobody will know about this?" he asked. "I mean, we came up here to my room."

"Oh, they'll know," she said, "but you're the Gunsmith. None of the men in this town are gonna think because I slept with you, I'll sleep with them."

"So you're saying this will be a one-time thing?"

She smiled slyly, a very pretty smile.

"Well, it may not be a one-time thing," she said, "but I believe it will be a one-man thing."

Clint stared at Ellie and for the first time since his arrival, since finding out that Rick was dead, he was feeling something other than rage.

"If you want me to leave, just say so," she told him.

"No," he said, unstrapping his gun, "I don't want you to leave." He walked to the bedpost and hung the gun up, then started to unbuckle his belt. "But if I'm taking my pants off, you've got to take something off, too."

"Oh honey," she said, reaching behind her, "I'm taking everything off."

In minutes they were both naked, standing on opposite sides of the bed.

"Ellie," he said, "I really need this."

She smiled, crawled onto the bed and said, "That makes two of us."

***

Cora came downstairs with the girls, who fanned out and began working right away. She went to the bar and accepted her glass of champagne from Otto.

"Has Clint come back?" she asked.

"He did, yeah," Otto said, "but there was somebody waitin' to see him."

"Who?"

"Ellie Howard."

"Ellie?" Cora asked, looking surprised. "What did she want?"

"I don't know for sure," Otto said, "but they went up to his room."

"How long ago?"

"Just a little while."

Cora looked up at the ceiling and sipped her champagne.

"Did you talk to her while she was here?" she asked.

"Only to tell her he wasn't here, and to take her drink order," Otto said. "I know Ellie, so we didn't really have anythin' to say to each other."

"Do you think she was sent here, or did she come on her own?"

"You're thinkin' Bennett might've sent her?"

"The thought occurred to me."

"But why?"

"I don't know," she said, "I'm just . . . suspicious."

"Maybe you should go up and rescue him," Otto said.

"Well," she said, "they might be doing something he doesn't want to get rescued from. So I guess we'll just wait and see when he comes back down."

***

Tillman entered the Blue Slipper and went right to the bar.

"What're you doin' here?" Auggie, the bartender, asked. "Ain't seen you in a dog's age."

"I'm lookin' for Eddie Dakota. You seen him, lately?"

"Not tonight, but he's been in here," Auggie said.

"If you see 'im, tell 'im I'm lookin' for him."

"Sure thing."

"What about Travis Biel," Tillman said. "You see 'im?"

"He's in the back, sittin' alone," Auggie said.

"That's good," Tillman said. "Gimme two beers."

Auggie set them up.

"Thanks," Tillman said.

He took the beers and walked to the back of the saloon, ignoring everybody he saw along the way. Travis Biel didn't see him until he was right next to him.

"Beer, Travis?"

The man looked up.

"That depends," Biel said. "What's it gonna cost me?"

"Ten minutes of your time."

"Siddown, then," Beil said, and reached for the fresh beer.

Chapter Nineteen

Ellie knew what she was doing in bed.

The minute they got between the sheets together her hands were all over him, and he returned the favor. While she stroked his chest, belly and crotch, he paid special attention to her full breasts and large nipples.

Clint needed to get lost in her opulent flesh for a short time, and he did his best, burying his face between her breasts then her thighs before finally mounting her and driving his hard cock into her. She was slick, hot and wet, and as they fucked, she implored him to go on and on, scratching his back and drumming her heels on his butt.

Afterwards they laid together on their backs, sweat cooling on their bare skin.

"I told you I knew it," she said. "We fit together real good."

"Yeah," he said, "a pretty good fit."

She turned her head to look at him.

"Have you found out who killed your friend?" she asked.

"Not yet," he said. "I'm still asking questions. Why? Do you know something?"

"No more than anybody else," she told him. "Just that Rick Hartman was shot and killed."

Now he turned his head to look back at her.

"You're a bartender in this town," he said. "Bartenders know everybody, hear everything. If you've got something to tell me, tell me now."

She rolled over and placed her hand on his chest.

"All I ever heard was talk that Hartman was getting too big too fast," she said. "Just idle talk, not from anybody who'd do anythin' about it."

"So who would do something about it, Ellie?" he asked. "The other saloon owners?"

"Not Charlie," she said. "He's happy with what he's got. But Rance . . ."

"What about Rance Edwards?"

She sat up and drew her knees up to her chest, wrapped her arms around them.

"He's more ambitious than Charlie, wants his place to be bigger," she said. "When the Palace opened . . . well, I think he knew he'd never be as big."

"You're giving him a reason to kill Rick, Ellie," Clint said.

"I don't know, Clint . . . Rance doesn't strike me as a killer."

"Who in town does?"

"Oh, there's men who would sell their guns," she said. "But you want the man who would hire them, right?"

"That's right."

"Well, that'd be a man with money."

"And who in town has the money?"

"A few men," she said, "including the mayor, a couple of ranchers, and some businessmen."

Clint turned his head, put his hands behind his head and stared at the ceiling.

"I guess I'm not helpin' much," she said.

He looked at her. "Not in the way you think," then grabbed her and pulled her on top of him. "Let's see if we can figure out another way."

***

Cora looked up when she saw Ellie coming down the stairs looking a bit frazzled.

"Ellie," she said, when Cora reached the bar.

"Cora."

"How are you doin'?" Cora asked.

"Pretty good."

"Let's talk," Cora said. "Champagne?"

"Why not?"

"Otto, two champagnes, Rick's table."

"Comin' up, Cora."

The two women walked to the back of the saloon, watched by the eyes of most of the men they passed.

They sat across from each other and Otto brought over two glasses and a bottle of champagne. He poured for them, and then left.

"Did you and Clint Adams get along?" Cora asked.

"Famously," Ellie said. "Does it matter to you? Do you have your eye on him?"

"No," Cora said, "he was Rick's friend, I'm just lookin' out for him."

"Well, believe me," Ellie said, "the man can look out for himself."

"Charlie didn't send you over here, did he, Ellie?"

"Charlie? Why on earth would he do that?"

"Maybe to find out what Clint knows about Rick's murder." Cora said.

"Charlie's not interested, Cora," Ellie said. "He's sorry Hartman's dead, but then he's not . . . you know what I mean?"

"And he had nothin' to do with it?"

"Not a thing," Ellie said. "He doesn't have the moxie for somethin' like that."

"So you came over here to see Clint for . . . what?"

Ellie drank down half her champagne and said, "Sex, pure and simple."

She put her glass down and stood up.

"Thanks for the drink, Cora."

Cora watched as Ellie walked to the batwing doors and left, then drank her own champagne and poured another.

Chapter Twenty

When Clint came down about fifteen minutes later, Cora was still sitting at Rick's table. He waved at Otto to bring him a beer and joined. The bartender brought him a frosty mug.

"Seems you and Ellie got along real well," Cora said.

"Is that a problem for you?" he asked.

"No, not for me," she said. "You can do what you want, but I thought you were lookin' for Rick's killer."

"I am," Clint said, "but I needed a short break from wanting to kill someone."

"I suppose I can understand that," Cora said.

"Do you have a problem with Ellie?"

"No, she's all right," Cora said.

"Is she?"

"What do you mean?"

"Do you think she's a liar?"

Cora smiled.

"No more than any other woman, I suppose. Why?"

"She told me she didn't know anything about Rick's death," Clint said.

"She told me the same thing."

"But in her opinion, there are a few men in town who would have the money to hire it done, including the mayor."

"Why would the mayor want Rick dead? This place is going to bring more people to Mission City. That's what the mayor wants."

"She mentioned there were some ranchers who could afford hired guns."

"Well, yeah, for a range war, or to catch cattle rustlers," Cora said. "Why would one of the rich ranchers want Rick Hartman dead?"

"I don't know," Clint said. "I guess I'll have to ride out and ask them."

"That's gonna take some time," she said.

"I'll go as fast or as slow as I have to in order to find the killer," he said, sipping his beer. "When I kill the man, I'll be sure I have the right one."

"I can't blame you for that," she said.

"You were going to get me a list of people who could afford to hire a gun."

"By last night," she said, putting her hand to her forehead. "I got busy with the girls. I'm sorry . . ."

"That's okay. Just make the list and include ranchers."

"I will, I promise," she said.

Clint finished his beer and stood up.

"I'm going to take a walk around town, talk to some of the storekeepers. One of them may have heard something."

"I suppose that's possible," she said.

"I'll see you here later, Cora."

"Sure, Clint."

He started to walk away, then turned back.

"Are we okay, Cora?"

"Why wouldn't we be, Clint?"

Satisfied, Clint turned and left the saloon.

***

During the afternoon he stopped in on what he considered to be some of the larger businesses in town. That included hotels, restaurants, the general store and some others. He asked the same questions of each owner. He asked how well they knew Rick Hartman, what they thought of Rick's Palace, and got the same answers. They liked the Palace, didn't know Rick all that well, and hadn't heard anything about somebody wanting to kill him.

As he started back to the Palace, he came across Sheriff Erickson.

"Sheriff."

"Adams," the lawman said. "How goes the investigation?"

"Slow," Clint said, "but that's what I figured. Seems nobody in town knows anything."

"Ain't that always the way?" Erickson asked. "Even if they knew, you think they'd tell you? You're a stranger in this town."

"And what about you? You're the law. Wouldn't they tell you? If you asked."

"Yeah, I'm the law," Erickson said. "That don't mean they'll talk to me, either."

"So you're happy to just go on, not knowing who killed him?" Clint asked.

"I wouldn't say I was happy about it, Adams," Erickson said, with a shrug. "That's just the way it is."

"Well," Clint said, "I can't accept that, Sheriff. So I guess I'll just go on asking questions."

"You got a whole town full of people," the lawman pointed out. "I guess that's gonna take some time."

"Not just in town," Clint said.

"Whataya mean?"

"I'm going to ride out and talk to some of the ranchers, see what they know," Clint said. "See how they feel about a murder in town."

"Which ranchers?" Erickson asked.

"I don't know, I suppose the biggest ones," Clint said. "The rich ones."

"You thinkin' one of them hired it done?" Erickson asked. "Why would they do that?"

"That's my question, Sheriff," Clint said, "the one I've been asking again, and again. Why would anyone want Rick Hartman dead? Sooner or later, I'm going to get my answer. Good day."

He walked past the sheriff, heading back to the Palace.

Chapter Twenty-One

As it turned out, Travis Biel knew where to find Eddie Dakota, and he arranged a meeting for the two of them with Tillman, later in the day. Instead of a saloon, they met in the same clearing where Tillman had met with Sheriff Erickson.

When the two of them rode up to the clearing, Tillman was waiting by a fire. He had a pot of coffee going, and a bottle of whiskey on the side to sweeten it.

"Step on down and have some coffee, boys," he said.

As they dismounted, the physical disparity between them became obvious. Eddie Dakota was a tall man—almost as tall as Tillman—while Travis Biel looked barely five-and-a-half feet tall. However, both wore a gun around their waist with the confidence of men who knew how to use them. The only other similarity between them was age, as both appeared to be in their thirties.

"Coffee?" Tillman asked.

"Why not?" Dakota said.

"Is that whiskey?" Biel asked, pointing.

"It is."

"Well, sweeten it up, man," Biel said.

Tillman poured three coffees, added whiskey and handed the cups out as Biel and Dakota hunkered down by the fire.

"Biel tells me you got a job for us," Dakota said. "Both of us?"

"Yeah," Tillman said, "but the job is more mine. What I need is some backup."

"Who or what are we backin' you up against?" Dakota asked.

"Clint Adams."

"What the hell," Dakota asked, "is the Gunsmith doin' in Mission City?"

"Seems somebody killed a friend of his, and he's bound and determined to find out who it was. I'm gettin' paid to get rid of him before that happens."

"Who was killed?" Dakota asked.

"Are we talkin' about Rick Hartman?" Biel asked, before Tillman could answer.

"That's who we're talkin' about," Tillman said.

"That's right," Dakota said, "I heard talk that they were friends."

"Well, they were," Tillman said. "Adams says he's gonna kill the man who killed Hartman, pure and simple."

"How's he gonna find out who did it?" Dakota asked.

"I don't know," Tillman said. "Looks like he's goin' around askin' questions."

They worked on their coffee for a while, each alone with his thoughts, before Tillman spoke again.

"Just between you, me and that tree over there, which one of you did it?" he asked.

Neither man looked shocked at the question.

"Hartman was shot in the back, right?" Dakota asked.

"That's right."

Dakota shook his head. "Not my style," he said.

"Mine, neither," Biel said. "What about you, Tillman?"

"I don't bushwhack people," Tillman said.

The three men exchanged a glance, knowing that it had to be one of them who did the job. Unless another money gun had been imported from outside.

"Okay, it don't matter," Tillman said. "I'm plannin' on facin' Adams head on, man-to-man. If he kills me, then I want you two to kill him."

"Backshoot 'im?" Biel asked.

"I ain't tellin' you how to do it," Tillman said.

"What if we wanna try 'im, too?" Dakota asked.

"You'll have to wait your turn," Tillman said. "I'm first, and if you fellas wanna try, you decide who's next."

"If the three of us faced him, he'd be done," Biel said. "And we'd still be the men who killed the Gunsmith."

"Yeah, but then we'd never know," Dakota said. "I mean, who was fastest. And which of us really killed 'im?"

"But we'd get paid," Biel said.

Dakota looked at Tillman.

"How much *are* we gettin' paid?" he asked. "For that matter, how much are you gettin'?"

"How much I'm gettin' is none of your business," Tillman said. "How much the two of you get is up for discussion."

"Well," Biel said, holding out his cup, "fill it up and let's discuss."

Dakota nodded and held out his cup, as well.

***

As both Biel and Dakota rode off, the deal having been struck, Tillman kicked dirt on the fire until it was out. Then he emptied the coffee pot remnants onto it for good measure and packed the pot and cups into his saddlebags. He swung up into the saddle with the bottle of whiskey in his hands. He took a healthy drink, then stowed that away in the saddlebags, as well.

They'd agreed on a price for each man, which came to a fraction of what he was going to charge. If he was going to risk his life in a showdown with the Gunsmith, somebody was going to pay big money for it.

Big money!

Chapter Twenty-Two

Clint decided to go and see if Cora had that list of names ready for him. Once he had a list, he'd start off the next morning, see how many he could cross off in one day of riding.

Rick's Palace was in full swing when he got back, with music blaring, the girls prancing and dancing around the floor—mostly to avoid grasping hands—and Cora standing at the bar, watching it all. Behind the bar Otto was busy serving drinks to customers, and to the girls, who were carrying them on trays to the seated customers. He watched for a few moments, amazed at how these girls managed to balance the drinks while avoiding being grabbed, and never spilling a drop.

He joined Cora at the bar, waved at Otto for a beer, when he had a chance.

"How'd it go?" she asked.

"Just as I expected," Clint said. "Nobody knows anything."

"Or they're just not sayin'," she said.

"Right. Erickson seemed to think nobody will talk to me because I'm a stranger."

"He may have a point."

"Well, tomorrow I'll start with the ranchers."

"That list!" she said and reached between her breasts. She came out with a piece of paper and handed it to Clint. "All the names I could think of. As for the ranchers, I included the names of their spreads. Anybody in town can tell you how to get to them."

"Thank you, Cora," he said, putting the list into his pocket.

"Clint, are you going to see Ellie again?"

"I don't know," he said. "Would it be a problem if I was?"

"Not a problem, per se," she answered. "I'd just be careful with her, she tends to have her own agenda."

"I think we all do," he said, "but thanks for the warning. I'll keep it in mind."

"Another beer?" Otto asked.

"No thanks. I'm going to turn in early tonight and get an early start in the morning."

"I'll have the coffee ready," Otto said.

"Much obliged," Clint said.

He bade good-night to all of them and went up to his room.

***

Tillman was sitting at a table alone across the room, watching Clint interact with Cora and Otto. Then he watched as Clint went up the stairs.

He could have challenged Clint Adams there and then, in front of a saloon full of witnesses, but he hadn't yet decided what his price was going to be. So he decided just to nurse a beer and scout the Gunsmith. He moved like a man at ease with himself, but Tillman could also see the rage in his stance. The man's own anger might just give him the edge he needed.

He stood up to leave and one of the girls, a pretty blonde, came over and said, "Leavin' already? I thought you were gonna buy me a drink?" She pouted.

"Another night, sweet thing," Tillman said. "I've got things to do."

"Well, come back when you have the time."

"Hey," he said, before she walked away, "maybe you can help me. Was that Clint Adams goin' up the stairs a few minutes ago?"

"Yeah, it was. He owns the place, now."

"I heard that," Tillman said, "but . . . does that mean he's livin' upstairs?"

"Yes, he has a room there," she said.

"I see."

"Why do you ask?"

Tillman shrugged.

"No reason. Just curious. The man's supposed to be a legend, you know."

"I know that," she said, "but he's also a real nice guy."

He chucked her under the chin with a finger and said, "I'll see you again, soon."

"I'll look forward to it."

He turned and left the saloon.

***

From across the room Otto saw Tillman drinking his beer and watching Clint Adams. He wondered what the man was doing in the Palace. He'd never seen him there before. He knew who he was, that he was a gun for hire. Now he watched him walk out of the saloon after talking to Melanie. He caught the girl's eye and called her over.

"What was that big fella talkin' to you about?" he asked.

"He was askin' about Clint. You know, because he's a legend and all."

"I see."

"Did I do somethin' wrong?"

"No, it's fine, Melanie," Otto said. "You can go on back to work."

Happy that she hadn't done anything wrong, she turned and flounced away, into the crowded interior of the saloon.

Chapter Twenty-Three

Clint came down the next morning for some of Otto's coffee before riding out to see the ranchers.

"'morning, Otto."

"'mornin', Clint. Coffee's ready. Have a seat."

The chair had been removed from the top of one table, and Clint sat. Otto brought him not only a pot and a cup but a basket of biscuits, with some butter and honey.

"What's all this?"

"You said you wanted to get an early start," Otto replied. "I thought you could have breakfast here."

"Thanks, Otto," Clint said. "That'll work for me. Why don't you sit down and join me?"

"Thanks," Otto said, sitting across from him. "I wanted to talk to you anyway."

"About what?"

Both men buttered a biscuit and took a bite.

"Do you know a man named Tillman?"

"Can't say I do," Clint said. "Why?"

"He was here last night, showing an interest in you."

"Showing an interest in what way?"

"He was asking Melanie about you and about where you live," Otto said.

"Do you know the man, Otto?"

"Most people around here do," Otto said. "He's a gun for hire."

"Ah . . . and why would he be interested in me, unless it had to do with Rick?"

"What if he just wants to try the Gunsmith?"

"There's always that," Clint said.

"If I was you, I'd watch my back."

"Otto, that's something I always do." He took a slip of paper from his pocket. "Now I have a favor to ask."

"What is it?"

"Cora gave me these names," Clint said. "I need to know how to get to their ranches."

Otto picked up the paper and looked at it.

"These are the three richest ranchers in the county," he said. "The main road out of town will take you to three of their spreads." Otto went on to tell Clint how to find his way to their houses from the main road.

"Thanks, Otto," Clint said. "Now how about telling me what you know about these men?"

"They've all been here to drink once or twice," Otto said. "Their men come in a lot, but some of them also frequent the Slipper and the Tree."

"How well did these men know Rick?"

"They knew him," Otto said. "I wouldn't say well."

"What else do you know about them?"

"You mean other than the fact that they're on the Town Council?"

"Wait a minute. They live outside of town. Aren't Council members usually townsmen? Men with businesses in town?"

"I guess that's how it usually is," Otto said, "but Mayor Pierpont set up his own Town Council and invited these three ranchers to be members."

"Is that it?" "Just the three of them?"

"No, there are two other members," Otto said, "and they do own businesses in town."

"Which businesses would those be?"

"The hotel, and the general store," Otto said.

"Ah, I spoke to the owner of the general store, a Mr. Howard Mantle. And I spoke to the owner of the Lexington Hotel, a Mr. William Brant. Both men claimed not to have any contact with Rick."

"Well," Otto said, "contact. They've also had drinks here and said hello to Rick. Is that contact?"

"It is."

"Then they lied."

"So they did," Clint said, "and I'm sure they're not the only ones who have lied."

Otto finished his second biscuit and washed it down with the last of his coffee. Then he stood.

"I better get this place ready for business today, boss," he said.

Clint finished his coffee and stood.

"Thanks for the information, Otto, and the warning."

"What are you going to do about Tillman?"

"I'll deal with him when I have to," Clint said. "I'm going to be away most of the day, but I'll be back tonight."

"I'll let Cora know."

"Good, and tell anyone else who's looking for me that I'm away," Clint said, "but don't tell them where."

"You got it."

"And thanks for breakfast."

Clint left the Palace and walked to the livery stable.

"You want your horse, Mr. Adams?" the hostler asked.

"I'll saddle him myself, thanks," Clint said.

He got the Tobiano saddled and walked him outside the stable before mounting up.

"Time to get you a little exercise, boy," he said, stroking the horse's neck. "Let's go."

Chapter Twenty-Four

The first ranch was the Grantchester Spread, owned by Arthur Grantchester. The house was large, two stories high, built mostly of logs. Clint dismounted in front of the house, looked around. There were no men in the corral or around the barn. He wondered where everyone was.

He went to the front door and knocked. The door was opened by a tall, thin man in his fifties wearing a white shirt, and trousers held up by suspenders.

"Yes?"

"Are you Mr. Grantchester?"

"I am."

"My name's Clint Adams."

"The Gunsmith," Grantchester said. "I heard you were around. Come on in."

Clint followed Grantchester to the front room, which was as far as the man took him. It was furnished in handmade furniture.

"Did you make all this?" Clint asked.

"Made the furniture, built the house," Grantchester ordered. "What can I do for you, Mr. Adams?"

"I'm trying to find out who killed Rick Hartman," Clint said.

"Then why are you here?"

"You're on the Town Council."

"I am."

"Did you have contact with Rick Hartman?"

"Only to say hello when I was in his place," Grant-chester said.

"You never did business with him?"

"What kind of business would I have with a saloon owner, beyond drinking?"

"Maybe trying to buy his place?"

"I own legitimate businesses, Mr. Adams."

"And you don't think a saloon is legitimate?"

"It's about as legitimate a business as a whorehouse is," the man said. "Anything else? I've got a day's work ahead of me."

"Where are all your men?"

"Out rounding up our horses," Grantchester said. "And I'm due out there."

Clint decided to try something else.

"Have you ever heard of a man named Tillman?"

"The gunman? Sure, most folks around here know him."

"Has he ever worked for you?"

"I hire ranch hands, not gunmen, Mr. Adams," Grantchester said. "I think you better go now. I've got to get moving."

"All right, Mr. Grantchester," Clint said. "Thanks for your time."

Grantchester walked him to the door.

"One more thing," Clint said.

"Yes?"

"I'm on my way to talk to the other members of the Council," Clint said. "Do you think any of them had business with Rick Hartman?"

"If they did, I'd know it. No, they didn't."

"Thanks for your time."

Clint went down the steps, mounted the Tobiano, and rode off, heading for the next ranch.

***

The second ranch was the Ricking-D, with the "D" lying on its side. It was more rustic than Grantchester's, only one story high. As he approached, he saw men in both the corral and the barn. They stopped working to study him as he rode up to the house.

As Clint dismounted, a man came walking over from the corral. He was a rough-hewn forty or so.

"Help ya?"

"I'm looking for the owner, Jordan Chance. Is that you?"

"No," the man said, "I'm Mr. Chance's foreman, Ken Wells. And you?"

"Clint Adams."

"I heard you was around town," Wells said. "Whataya doin' out here?"

"I want to ask Mr. Chance some questions."

"What about?"

"Murder."

"What? Who? Oh, wait a minute," Wells said. "You're talkin' about Rick Hartman."

"That's right."

"Mr. Jordan don't know nothin' about that."

"I'd like to hear that from him."

"You're hearin' it from me," Wells said. "You're gonna leave Mr. Chance alone."

"What about you, then?"

"What about me?"

"You know anything about the murder?"

"I think you oughtta leave, Adams," Wells said, bunching his hands into fists. He had no weapon on him, so Clint didn't feel threatened.

At that point, the front door of the house opened, and an old man appeared, leaning on a cane.

"What's goin' on, Ken?" he yelled.

"This fella was just leavin', Mr. Chance."

"Mr. Chance, my name is Clint Adams," Clint shouted. "I'd like to talk to you about Rick Hartman."

"I told you—" Wells started, but the old man cut him off.

"For chrissake, Ken, just let the fella in!"

"You heard the man," Wells said.

Chapter Twenty-Five

Clint went up the walk to the front door and entered the house. He was immediately struck by how dark and musty the house was.

"In here," Chance said. It was a short walk to an even mustier sitting room, where the old man lowered himself into a leather chair.

"Sit anywhere," he said. "It's all dusty. I ain't been out of the house in years, and every so often I have a woman come in and clean, but she ain't been here in a while."

Clint sat on a rickety looking wooden chair.

"I let you in because I ain't talked to anybody in months, so this better be good."

"I understood you were on the Town Council," Clint said. "Don't you go to meetings?"

"No," Chance said, with a dismissive wave. "The mayor has my proxy. I go along with anythin' he wants."

"Well, I'm here about the murder of Rick Hartman."

"That's the fella who owns the Palace?" Chance asked. "Yeah, my foreman told me about that. Shot in the back, was it? Damn shame!"

"It's going to be a damn shame for whoever did it, when I catch up to them," Clint said.

"Then why are you here?" Chance asked. "Why ain't you out lookin'?"

"I am out lookin', Mr. Chance," Clint said.

"Here?" The man laughed. "If you think I had anythin' to do with it, you're barkin' up the wrong tree."

"I'm talking to all of the ranchers who are rich enough to have hired a killer."

"I'm rich, all right." He banged his cane on the floor. "For all the good it does me. I still ain't gettin' a new hip, or a new heart."

"I'm sorry to hear that."

"Don't be," Chance said. "I've lived a long life and, as you said, I'm rich. So you're thinkin' somebody hired a killer to backshoot your friend?"

"I'm thinking it was paid for, yes," Clint said. "The backshooting part might just have been the killer's choice. Which means he probably won't face me when I find him."

"Look, Adams, I don't go for backshootin' a man," Chance said. "If I did it myself, I'd be face-to-face. If I hired it done, I'd want it done that way, too. But I didn't do either one of those things. There was nothin' in it for me. You might as well check with the other ranchers."

"I already talked to Mr. Grantchester."

Chance laughed.

"Now there's a sonofabitch if I ever met one," the old man said. "But he don't hire gunmen."

"Are you sure?"

"Positive," he said. "I've known him for almost forty years. Never knew him to hire a gun." He waved a gnarled hand. "Look elsewhere, my friend."

"Then I guess I better keep looking," Clint said, standing.

"Before you do that, can you do me a favor?"

"What's that?"

"Have a whiskey with me," Chance said.

"Why not?"

"Good," Chance said. "There's a bottle over there on that sideboard. You pour. It's painful for me to walk."

Clint went and got two whiskeys, brought one back to the old man and handed it to him.

"Ahhh," Chance said, his eyes lighting up. "You go ahead and toss yours back. I'm gonna sip and savor. I allow myself one a day, and the doctor says I shouldn't even have that."

"What do doctors know?" Clint said.

"Exactly how I feel!"

"To your health," Clint said, and tossed it back.

"What's left of it," Chance said and sipped.

***

When Clint came out of the house, the foreman was waiting by his horse.

"Is he okay?" he asked.

"He's fine, as far as I can see."

"Did he make you get him a glass of whiskey?"

"He didn't force me," Clint said. "He asked me to have one with him, and I did."

"That old coot."

"Was he telling me the truth about not being out of the house in years?"

"Oh yeah," Wells said, much less aggressive than he was before. "He's got a bad heart and bad hip, can't ride, and doesn't see the point of comin' out."

"That's too bad," Clint said. "I get the impression he was once a robust man."

"He was," Wells said, "but those days are gone. Now he has me come in every night and tell him about the day."

"So that's how you told him about Rick Hartman's murder?"

"That's right."

Clint unwrapped the Tobiano's reins from the hitching post and mounted up.

"So whataya think, Adams?" Wells smiled, holding back a laugh. "Is he your killer?"

"I think I'm crossing him off my list," Clint said, and rode away.

Chapter Twenty-Six

The third ranch was the Double-R. The operation looked much less rustic or handmade than the other two. His guess was that the owner, Rex Randolph, had professional carpenters come in and build the house, barn and corral.

There were a few ranch hands at the corral as he rode up to the one-story house and dismounted. The front door opened and a woman, dressed like a man in jeans and a work shirt, stepped out and regarded him curiously. He looked around to see if any of the men were approaching, and they weren't. They were all just watching. Finally, the woman stepped from the porch and came toward him. She was about forty, tall and attractive, with dark hair that fell to her shoulders.

"Can I help you?" she asked. She was holding a pair of gloves in her hands.

"Yes, I'm looking for Mr. Randolph."

"That would be my husband," she said.

"Can I speak to him?"

"I'm afraid he's been dead for several months."

"I see. I'm sorry. Who runs the ranch now?"

"I do," she said. "That's why they're all watching to see what I do."

Clint looked over at the corral again, saw all the men—about half a dozen of them—watching.

"They're waiting for one misstep, so they can quit, like the others."

"The others?"

"While my husband was alive, we had thirty hands," she said. "Now I have those six."

"Do you have a foreman?"

"No, he was the first one to leave after Rex died. Can I ask what your business is?"

"I'm looking into the murder of Rick Hartman," he said. "I understood your husband was on the Town Council."

"He was. Now I am, but I don't go to meetings. The mayor has my proxy. Who are you?"

"My name's Clint Adams."

"I heard you were in town," she said, holding her gloves in her right hand and slapping them into her left. "All right, you'd better come in, then."

Clint tied his horse to the hitching post and followed her into the house. It was cleaner, brighter and better furnished than either of the other two houses he'd seen.

"A drink?" she asked.

"Yes, thanks."

"Whiskey or brandy?"

"Whiskey," he said.

"A man after my own heart," she said. "The brandy was my husband's. He was much older than me, and his tastes showed it."

She poured two glasses and carried them over to him. Up close he could see how tall she really was, especially in her boots. She almost matched his six feet.

"Cheers," she said.

"Cheers."

They both drank.

"Now suppose you tell me what I can do for you?" she said. "About this murder?"

"It's come to my attention that Rick Hartman's murder may have been paid for."

"By who?"

"That's what I'm trying to find out."

She tapped her fingernail on her glass for a few moments.

"And you thought my husband might have a reason to do that?" she asked.

"Possibly."

"What possible reason could there be?" she asked.

"Well, for instance . . . you're a beautiful woman, and Rick was kind of a ladies' man."

"You think I'd risk my marriage for a fling?" she asked, looking amused. "And if I had a fling, my husband would have the man killed?"

"It's been known to happen."

"Are you questioning other men who have beautiful wives?" she asked.

"No," he said, "this just occurred to me when I saw you."

"Well, as I said, Rex has been dead for months. He died of a heart attack. So I guess that strikes him off your list."

"I guess it does."

"And I'm a little busy trying to keep this ranch afloat, to be bothered with anything that's going on in town."

"I can see that." He set his glass down on a nearby table. "I suppose I owe you an apology for taking up your time."

"Not at all," she said, walking him to the door. "It was an interesting distraction from my day."

She not only walked him to the door, but out to his horse.

"You just caught me as I was going out to talk to what's left of my hands," she said. She looked over. "Ah, I see I still have six."

"I hope everything goes okay for you, Mrs. Randolph."

"Rachel," she said, "you can call me Rachel. I think my husband married me so that when he died, the name of the ranch wouldn't have to be changed."

"He sounds like a man who looked ahead."

Clint mounted Toby, looked over at Rachel Randolph, who was walking to the corral where her men were waiting, then rode off.

Chapter Twenty-Seven

Talking with the three wealthiest ranchers in the county had yielded Clint very little. He didn't feel that any of them had the motive to have Rick Hartman killed.

He realized when he had told Rachel Randolph that Rick was a ladies' man, he had not discussed that point with Cora. He didn't know if she'd be offended or not, but he was going to have to ask about Rick and other women. A jealous husband would certainly shoot a rival in the back. Jealousy robbed men of all logic and sense.

He rode back into Mission City before dusk, left the Tobiano at the livery and walked to Rick's Palace. It was well lit and lively, as usual. Rick Hartman was always the kind of man who knew how to put together a profitable business, and this seemed to be no exception.

Clint didn't see Cora anywhere, so he went to the bar and elbowed in. Otto spotted him and came over right away.

"Sheriff Erickson was lookin' for you today," the bartender said.

"What about?" Clint asked.

"He said he wanted to be the one to tell you," Otto said, "but I heard they had somebody in a cell who came in and confessed to killing Rick."

Clint was out the door in seconds . . .

***

He ran into the sheriff's office, slamming the door behind him.

"Where is he?" he demanded.

Erickson looked up from his desk.

"I see somebody let the cat out of the bag," he said.

"Never mind," Clint said. "Where is he? Who is he?"

"He's in cell," Erickson said. "His name's Abe Ripley."

"Why did he do it?"

"He says he was drunk," Erickson said, "and he's not sure why he did it."

"I want to talk to him."

"I figured," Erickson said, grabbing the cell block keys. "Come on."

He led the way back to the center of three cells, where a man sat on a cot with his head in his hands.

"Abe, somebody to see you," Erickson said.

"Unlock the cell," Clint said.

"I can't do that, Adams," Erickson said. "You'd kill 'im. You can talk to him from right here." The lawman looked at Clint's gun. "I don't suppose you'd give me your gun?"

"No!"

"Well, I guess you're not in the habit of shootin' un-armed men through a cell door," Erickson said. "I'll be in the office."

Erickson left the cell block.

"Hey! Ripley!"

The man didn't move.

"Abe Ripley! Look at me!"

Slowly, he lifted his head. Clint saw a sad, haggard face, ravaged by years of drinking. If this man was any-thing, he was the town drunk.

"Did you kill Rick Hartman?" Clint asked.

Ripley stared at him and just nodded miserably.

"Why?"

Slowly, Ripley said, "I—I don't know."

"Where's the gun you used?" Clint asked.

"I—I don't know."

This man could not have killed Rick, Clint thought.

"Do you remember shooting him?" Clint asked. "Or did somebody tell you that you did it?"

"I—I don't remember," Ripley said. "I don't re-member nothin'. Can I—can I have a drink?"

"Sure, I'll get you all the whiskey you want," Clint said, "just tell me who told you that you shot Rick Hartman?"

Ripley looked forlorn and said, "I—I don't remember," figuring he'd never get a drink now.

"I'll be back," Clint said, and left the block.

Erickson looked up from his desk as Clint came out.

"I didn't hear a shot," he said. "Are you satisfied?"

"That sad excuse for a man didn't shoot Rick Hartman," Clint said.

"He told me he did."

"No," Clint said, "somebody told *him* he did."

"Why would somebody do that?" Erickson asked.

"To get me to stop looking," Clint said. "I'm going to get him some whiskey. If he has a drink, he might remember who told him to confess."

"Look, you—" Erickson said, but Clint didn't give him a chance to finish. He was out the door, in search of a bottle of whiskey.

***

Instead of going to a saloon for the whiskey, Clint stopped in the general store and bought a bottle. It wasn't long before he reentered the sheriff's office with the bottle.

"I'm not gonna give you the key, Adams," Erickson said.

"I'll just hand him the bottle through the bars," Clint said. "And we'll have our answer soon."

He went into the cell block to the center cell, where Ripley was now lying down on the cot, his back to the door.

"Ripley!" Clint called. "Hey, Ripley! Whiskey!"

The man didn't move.

"Come on, Ripley, wake up!" Clint shouted.

Still nothing.

"Sheriff!" Clint called.

"What's goin' on?" Erickson asked.

"Something's wrong," Clint said. "Open the cell."

"Lemme get the key."

Erickson went back to the office, then came in with the key.

"I dunno what you're tryin' to pull," he said.

"He's not moving," Clint said.

"Abe! Hey, Abe!" the sheriff yelled. "Shit!"

Hastily, Erickson unlocked the cell door, opened it and rushed in, followed by Clint.

"Abe, come on!" Erickson said, grabbing the man's shoulder.

He turned Ripley onto his back, and it was obvious the man was dead.

Chapter Twenty-Eight

"Did you do this?" Clint demanded.

"What?"

"Did you kill him so he couldn't talk to me?"

"Why the hell would I kill 'im?" Erickson said. "And you weren't even gone that long."

"Gone long enough for somebody to put a pillow over his face and suffocate him."

"Do you see a pillow around here?" Erickson asked. "I'm not in the habit of makin' prisoners comfortable. This ain't a damned hotel."

Erickson checked the body while Clint watched.

"Not a mark on him," the lawman said.

"Look at his face, and his tongue," Clint said. "He was suffocated, I tell you."

"From where?" Erickson asked. "Outside the cell. From that window? Listen, Abe was the town drunk. I think he just . . . died."

"I'm not accepting that," Clint said. "I'm not accepting that he shot Rick, or that he died before he could tell me who put him up to confessing."

"But you'd accept that I killed 'im?"

"Either that or you let whoever killed him in," Clint said.

Erickson stormed past Clint out of the cell and back into his office.

"Look, I've gotta deal with this, now," he said. "I'll have to get the undertaker to come and get him."

"And have a doctor examine him," Clint said.

"What for?"

"I want to know if somebody killed him, or he just . . . died."

"I can get the town doctor over to the undertaker's," Erickson said.

"I'll stay here while you go make arrangements," Clint said.

"Why are you gonna stay here?"

"Because I don't want the body to mysteriously disappear."

"Why would it—oh hell," Erickson said. "Fine. Stay here til I get back."

The sheriff grabbed his hat and went out the front door. Clint went to the window, and watched the lawman walk down the street. Then he went back to the cell block to make his own study of the dead body.

Erickson was right. There wasn't a mark on Ripley. But he was sure the doctor would find that the man had been suffocated and had not died from natural causes.

And it seemed the only man who could have done it was the sheriff.

He found the rear door to the cell block, opened it and stepped out. The rear of the building was just a back alley, with nothing in it. An examination of the door showed that it had a broken lock.

He went back inside, figured while the sheriff was gone, he might as well take advantage and have a look through his desk. He sat down and went through the drawers. There were wanted posters, a bottle of whiskey, a dirty coffee mug, some extra bullets, papers that didn't seem to have anything to do with the town, just personal letters.

He closed all the drawers and stood up. A prowl around the office revealed nothing as well—nothing about Rick's murder, nothing about Abe Ripley.

Erickson either killed Ripley or let somebody else in to do it. There was no other way of looking at it.

When the door opened, the sheriff walked in with the undertaker, Tate.

"Where's the doctor?" Clint asked.

"On the way."

"I'll look at the body—" Tate started, but Clint stopped him.

"Let's wait for the doctor."

Chapter Twenty-Nine

The physician was Doctor George Sheridan, a tall man in his forties who came rushing in moments later.

"What've we got, Sheriff?"

"Looks like a dead prisoner."

"We want to know how he died," Clint said, "before we move him."

The doctor looked at Clint.

"Doc Sheridan, this is Clint Adams."

"Ah," Sheridan said, "I heard you were in town. Where's the body?"

"The center cell," Erickson said.

"I'll show you," Clint said.

"Lead the way, Mr. Adams."

Clint took Doc Sheridan to the cell but didn't enter with him. He watched as the sawbones examined the body.

"Well, he's dead, all right," Sheridan said, looking at Clint over his shoulder.

"Can you tell how he died?"

"I can do a more thorough examination later," Sheridan said, standing up, "but it looks to me like he was suffocated."

"So he was murdered."

"That's my assessment right here and now, yes," Sheridan said.

"You mind telling the sheriff that?"

"Not at all."

They went back out to the office together, where Erickson and Tate were waiting.

"Well?" Erickson said.

"Somebody killed him."

"Damn it!" Erickson said. "How?"

"He was suffocated."

Erickson looked at Clint.

"May I take him now?" Tate asked.

"I'd say yes," Sheridan said, "but I'd like to do another, more thorough exam at your shop. Is that all right?"

"If you help me carry him there," Tate said.

"Deal," Sheridan said.

"Anythin' else, Sheriff?" Tate asked.

"Take 'im," Erickson said. "I don't want 'im here."

Clint and Erickson watched as Tate and Sheridan carried the body out the front door. Then Erickson sat at his desk.

"Okay," Clint said, "so what happened? He was alive when I left."

"I didn't move from this spot."

"Your back door has a broken lock," Clint said. "You didn't hear anybody come in?"

"Not a sound."

"There had to be something," Clint said. "How would someone get into the cell to kill him, unless you let him in?"

Erickson stood up quickly.

"You're accusin' me of killin' him, or helpin' to kill him?"

"Do you have another suspect?"

"Get out of here, Adams!" Erickson shouted." Go out and find who killed your friend."

"That's just it, Sheriff," Clint said. "Whoever put Ripley up to confessing, and then killed him also killed Rick Hartman."

"You're still lookin' at me," Erickson said, "and I don't like it."

"I can't say I like it much myself," Clint said. "I'll see you around."

Clint turned and stormed out of the office.

***

When he got to the undertaker's office, Tate was out front, while Sheridan was in the back doing his final exam.

"Who's payin' for Ripley's burial?" Tate asked.

"You better talk to the sheriff about that," Clint said. "He was killed while he was in custody."

"Right," Tate said. "By the way, your friend's new coffin is ready."

"And the headstone?"

"That's gonna be a couple of days yet."

"Where's the body?"

"It's on ice," Tate said, "but it's gonna have to go into the ground as soon as the headstone's ready."

"Got it," Clint said. "Can I go back there and talk to the doc?"

"Sure."

Clint passed through the curtained doorway, saw the doctor bent over the body on a table.

"Can we talk while you do that?" Clint asked.

The man turned around.

"I'm done," he said. "He was murdered."

"Did you also examine the body of Rick Hartman?" Clint asked.

"I did, but that was open-and-shut. Two bullets in the back. Death was instantaneous."

"Doc, did you know Rick well?"

"No," Sheridan said. "I drank in his place once or twice, said hello, but I can't say I knew him."

"Would you have any idea who'd want to kill him?"

"Not a clue," the doctor said. "I thought his place would be good for this town. I can't see why anybody would want to kill him, unless it was just for personal reasons that had nothing to do with his business."

"And what could be that personal?"

"I don't know," Sheridan said. "A jealous husband or boyfriend, maybe."

"That's what I've started thinking."

"I've heard it said around town that you intend to kill whoever killed him."

"That's right, I do."

"And do you think the same person killed Ripley, here?"

"Got to be. They forced Ripley to confess, thinking I'd accept it, but he couldn't pull it off, so they killed him."

"Are you looking at Sheriff Erickson?"

"I can't see anyone else," Clint said. "I left him alone in the office with Ripley for . . . fifteen minutes. All he had to do was go into the cell, or let somebody in."

"Can you prove it?"

"No," Clint said, "not yet."

"Well," the sawbones said, "I wish you luck, then. I've got to get back to my office."

"Thanks for your time, Doc."

Chapter Thirty

Clint needed a drink, but instead of going to Rick's Palace, he went to the Bent Tree, where Ellie was the bartender. It was after dark, and he knew all the saloons would be busy, but the Bent Tree was the quietest.

"Look who's here," she said, with a smile, as he approached the bar.

"I need a beer," he said.

"Yes, sir!" she said.

She drew one and set it down in front of him.

"Rough day?"

"Very."

"Bad news?"

"Do you know a man named Abe Ripley?"

"Ripley?" she said. "Sure, he's the town drunk. I give him a drink now and then. He's harmless."

"He's dead."

"What?" She was startled. "How?"

"Somebody killed him, while he was in a jail cell."

"Was he sleepin' one off?" she asked.

"No," Clint said, "he was in jail because he confessed to killing Rick Hartman."

"What? That's crazy."

"I know," he said. "I spoke with him, and knew he'd been put up to it."

"By who?"

"I don't know."

"Didn't he say?"

"He couldn't remember," Clint said. "I thought a drink might jog his memory, so I went to get a bottle of whiskey. When I came back, he was dead."

"Oh my God. Who did it?"

"Whoever killed Rick."

"But . . . he was in a cell."

"And it was locked," Clint said. "It would take a key to get in and kill him."

"So . . . the sheriff?"

"That's what I'm thinking, but I can't prove it."

"So now you're tryin' to solve two murders?"

"I am," Clint said, "but I think I'm still looking for one killer."

"This sounds like it's gettin' harder and harder," she said.

"I never thought it'd be easy," Clint said, "but now I've got somebody working against me, trying to cover it up."

"I'm sorry," she said. "I wish I could help."

"You did," Clint said. "You helped me think about something else for a while."

"Well," she said, leaning her elbows on the bar, "I could help like that again."

"I don't think so."

"No?" She stood up straight.

"Oh, not that I wouldn't want to," he hurriedly said. "But I don't think I should be distracted until I've finished what I started."

"I suppose I can understand," she said. "I just hope it's soon."

"So do I." He put a coin on the bar. "Thanks for the beer."

"Come again," she said, "soon."

He smiled and left, this time heading back to the Palace.

***

It was crowded and noisy, and he didn't want to stop at the bar. He just walked through the saloon to the stairs and went up to his room. He thought about reading, but he didn't do that for the same reason he didn't sleep with Ellie again. It would distract him from what he really should be thinking about.

Who killed Rick and Ripley?

Chapter Thirty-One

Tillman was set.

He was going to call the Gunsmith out, making it look like just another gun making a try at a legend, rather than someone being paid to kill him. He was going to have Eddie Dakota on one side of the street, and Travis Biel on the other side, just to cover him.

He woke that morning and had himself a huge steak-and-eggs breakfast, washed it down with several cups of coffee sweetened with whiskey. The food and coffee was to satisfy his hunger, the whiskey was to bolster his resolve. When he stepped out of the café door, he was ready.

He walked down the street to an alley that ran alongside the hardware store. He found Dakota and Biel waiting for him there, as planned.

"When are we doin' this?" Dakota asked.

"You nervous?"

"Hell yeah, we're nervous," Biel said. "This is the Gunsmith we're talkin' about."

"Relax," Tillman said.

Dakota peered closely at Tillman.

"You been drinkin'?" he asked.

"Just sweetened my mornin' coffee a bit," Tillman said. "Don't worry about it."

"Where *is* Adams, anyway?" Biel asked.

"He's got a room in the Palace," Tillman said. "He's gotta come out sometime. Or, if he hasn't come out by the time they open for business, I'll go in and get 'im."

"Alone?" Dakota asked.

"You fellas can come in with me if ya want," Tillman said, "but I'll be callin' him out into the street. I want the whole town to see this."

"You really think you can beat 'im?" Biel asked.

"He's been a legend for a long time," Tillman said. "You know what? The longer a legend is around, the more they rust."

"Rust don't mean slow," Dakota pointed out.

"Look," Tillman said, "if he beats me, you two just have to get the job done. After all, we're bein' paid to kill 'im."

"You're bein' paid to kill 'im," Dakota pointed out. "We're bein' paid by you, to back your play."

"Fine, fine," Tillman said. "Put it any way you can deal with it."

"When's the Palace open?" Dakota asked.

"In a couple of hours," Tillman said. "You guys need to be patient. How about a drink while we wait?"

***

Clint came down and had coffee with Otto. He remembered doing this quite often with Rick Hartman in Labyrinth, Texas.

"Seems to me this murder business is gettin' harder-and-harder to figure," the bartender said.

"Otto, you're the bartender at the biggest and, dare I say, best saloon in town. Who've you seen Abe Ripley talking with?"

"To tell you the truth, Clint," Otto said, "we didn't let Ripley come in here. Rick said that wasn't the image we wanted to put out there."

"Can't blame him for that," Clint said. "You don't need the town drunk hangin' around."

"You should check the Blue Slipper and the Bent Tree."

"What the hell kind of name is 'The Blue Slipper' for a saloon?" Clint wondered aloud.

"You'd have to ask Rance Edwards about that," Otto said.

"You know," Clint said, "I just might do that. I went to the Bent Tree last night. Ellie said she gave Ripley drinks from time to time, and she thought he was harmless."

"She'd do that," Otto said. "Ellie's a nice kid."

"She agrees with me," Clint said. "Somebody put that poor drunk up to confessing."

"That's a surprise," Otto said, his eyebrows going up. "What about Tillman? What're ya gonna do about him?"

"I'll wait for him," Clint said.

"To shoot you in the back?"

"If Tillman's a money gun, he'll come straight at me, face-to-face," Clint said. "I'll find out who hired him or kill him . . . or both. It's going to be up to him."

"Tillman's fast, Clint."

"Nobody's going to outdraw me while I'm looking for Rick's killer, believe me."

Otto did.

***

When Clint came out of the Palace, Tillman, Dakota and Biel were across the street.

"There he is," Tillman said. "I won't have to go inside to get 'im. You two get into position."

Dakota stayed where he was, while Biel crossed to the other side. It was early, the street wasn't busy, and businesses were just opening. The sound of merchants sweeping up in front of their shops could be heard up and down the street.

"Clint Adams!" Tillman shouted, and that's all it took. The sweeping stopped, and doors slammed.

Chapter Thirty-Two

Clint heard the voice and looked across the street. A tall man stepped into view.

"You must be Tillman," he said.

"Oh, you've heard of me?"

"Just yesterday, for the first time," Clint said. "I've been expecting you."

The street had emptied out in anticipation of what was to come, but for two men.

"I see you brought help," Clint said.

"Not help," Tillman said. "Back up. Fellas like you and me, we need to have somebody watchin' our backs." Tillman looked around. "Only I see you're alone."

"You're right, I should have somebody watching my back," Clint said. "People get shot in the back in this town."

"Not by me," Tillman said. "That ain't my way."

"I can see that," Clint said.

"This is how I like it," Tillman said.

"And I assume if I kill you, your two friends will draw their guns."

"That's gonna be up to them."

"Oh, no," Clint said, "I think they know what they're getting paid for. What I'd like to know from you is, who's paying you."

"What makes you think somebody's payin' me?"

"There's too much going on in this town for somebody with money not to be behind it," Clint said. "You're being paid, all right."

"I don't think you should worry about who's payin'," Tillman said. "I think you should worry about who's in front of you."

"Oh, I'm not worried about that, Tillman," Clint said. "See, I'm going to find out who's behind all of this, and nobody can stop me."

"Are you believin' your own legend, Adams?" Tillman asked.

"Why don't you shut up and just do what you came to do," Clint said.

Tillman didn't speak again. He went for his gun, hoping to catch the Gunsmith just a split second off guard. He felt sure that with that slight advantage, he could outdraw Clint Adams, and kill him.

Unfortunately for Tillman, that advantage did not exist. Clint Adams had stayed alive for many years because he was always ready, because he knew that a split second could be the difference.

So he was not in the habit of giving even a second away.

***

Dakota and Biel watched as Tillman staggered back from the impact of not one, but two bullets. There was a moment's hesitation, and then the tall man fell onto his back, his gun still in his holster.

They both looked at Clint Adams, who remained standing in the street, as if waiting for something. Then they realized he was waiting for them to react.

Dakota and Biel exchanged a glance across the street. While Dakota wasn't sure what he wanted to do—turning and walking away was a *big* option—Biel went ahead and made the decision for them.

He turned and ran.

***

Clint saw the two men who were supposed to be backing Tillman's play exchange a glance, and then one ran. Clint then turned and looked at the second man.

"No, no," the man said, putting his hands out, "don't shoot."

Clint, with gun still in his hand walked to the man.

"Toss your gun aside," he said. "With the left hand."

143

The man reached across his body, plucked his gun from his holster and tossed it. Clint then quickly ejected his two spent shells, reloaded, and replaced his own weapon in his holster.

"What's your name?" he asked.

"Eddie Dakota."

"Who hired you, Eddie?" Clint said. "Who paid you and your friend to back Tillman?"

"Tillman was gonna pay us."

"You haven't been paid yet?"

"No, sir."

"Who was paying Tillman?"

"He-he never said. Honest."

"And what were you supposed to do?" Clint asked.

"Just back his play."

"But you didn't."

"We—we didn't even see you draw," Dakota said, "and Tillman's gun is still in his holster."

"So you both decided to run?"

"I—I guess so."

"What's your friend's name?"

"Biel, Travis Biel."

"So Biel ran," Clint said. "Why didn't you?"

"Um," Dakota said, looking down at his feet, "I couldn't."

"What the hell happened here?" a voice called.

Clint turned and saw Sheriff Erickson approaching.

Chapter Thirty-Three

Once again Sheriff Erickson had a body carried to the undertaker's office, and then took Clint and Eddie Dakota to his office to get the story.

"Well," the lawman said, "I can't say I'm sorry to see Tillman go. I never knew when he was gonna decide to gun somebody."

"Didn't he usually do it when he got paid?" Clint asked.

"Oh, his gun was for hire, but he also had a habit of gunning men down for his own amusement. That's when he wasn't beatin' on some man or woman—usually a whore."

"Sounds like I did this town a favor," Clint said.

"Hey!" Eddie Dakota shouted from a cell. "You can't keep me in here. I didn't do nothin'."

"He's right," Erickson said, "all I've got him for right now is watchin' you gun Tillman."

"Then you better let him out of that cell before somebody decides to kill him," Clint suggested.

"And why don't you get outta here before I decide to toss *you* into a cell," the lawman snapped.

"And then I'd end up dead, for sure," Clint said.

Erickson scowled and went into the cell block to release Dakota.

Clint decided to wait for the man outside.

The door of the sheriff's office opened, Dakota stepped out, strapping on his gun. When he saw Clint, he stopped short.

"I ain't gonna face you, Adams," he said, letting the gunbelt dangle from his left hand.

"Go ahead, strap it on, Dakota," Clint said. "I just want to talk."

"About what?" Dakota said. "I tol' ya what I know. We wuz supposed to back Tillman, and we wasn't paid yet."

"You always do jobs like that before you get paid?" Clint asked.

"When it's Tillman, yeah," Dakota said. "He was reliable and usually paid what he owed."

"So now neither you or your friend Biel is going to get paid," Clint said. "But I guess that's okay, since neither of you did the job you were supposed to do."

"Hey, once you gunned Tillman before he cleared leather, I didn't want nothin' to do with you."

"Okay, Eddie," Clint said, "if you can't tell me anything, I guess we're done."

"I can go?"

"Sure, why not?"

"You—you ain't gonna gun me?"

"I'm not Tillman," Clint said. "I don't gun men down for my own enjoyment. But you better get moving before I change my mind."

Dakota ran off down the street, still trying to get his gunbelt buckled.

Clint stared at the door of the sheriff's office. For some reason Erickson didn't feel like a killer to him. But that didn't mean the lawman didn't know who had killed Rick, or that he hadn't let somebody into the cell to kill Ripley. But the man *did* strike Clint as the puppet type. All he had to do was find out who was pulling the strings.

He thought about going back into the office and laying his hands on the sheriff, but Erickson was still a lawman, and Clint could end up in a cell, waiting for somebody to kill *him*.

So he turned and walked away.

***

Erickson looked out the window of his office and saw Clint Adams still standing there. He waited impatiently for the man to finally walk away, then hurriedly left his office.

It was a matter of a few streets before he got to the building he wanted and went inside.

"What's going on?" the man behind the desk asked. "You're out of breath."

"There's too much goin' on," Erickson said. "First Hartman, then Ripley, now Tillman's dead."

"What? You told me he'd do the job."

"He foolishly tried to take Adams face-to-face," Erickson said. "He never got his gun out of his holster."

"Goddamnit!" the man swore. "This is still your job, Erickson. Get rid of Adams."

"How?"

"I don't care. Send half a dozen men after him. Have him shot down in the street. At the very least, that would put us on the map, like Tombstone and Dodge."

"You wanna be that kind of town?" Erickson asked.

"I want the Gunsmith out of the way," the man said. "Then we'll worry about what kind of town we are. Do you understand me, Sheriff?"

"I understand."

"Then get the hell out of my office and get the god-damned job done!"

Chapter Thirty-Four

Clint watched Erickson leave the building, glad that he had decided to double back and follow him. Now he just had to find out who had an office in there.

He went through the front door, found himself in a lobby, standing in front of a stairway. It looked like a fairly new building, two-story brick, with offices on both floors. Which one had Erickson gone into?

He walked around, found a list on the wall of the offices that were in the building. It looked like there were eight, but only four of them were occupied. He wasn't in City Hall, so he didn't expect any of the offices to be the mayor's, and they weren't. Two of them were listed as attorneys, one had the word "investments" after the name, and the fourth listing was just a name.

He decided his only option was to visit all four and see how the occupants reacted.

Two of the offices were on the first floor, and two on the second. He started with the first.

Listed in room 101 was Andrew Murphy, Attorney-at-Law. He opened the door without knocking. There was an outer office, apparently for a secretary, but it was deserted. With not even a desk.

"In here!" a man called from the next room.

Clint crossed the room and entered. A man in shirt-sleeves was seated behind a desk covered with folders and papers. He looked up at Clint who saw that he was roughly fifty years old.

"Sorry," the man said, "my secretary left and, as you can see, she took her desk with 'er. What can I help you with?"

"Uh, I was looking for the sheriff, and someone told me he came in here?"

"To see me?" the man who was obviously Andrew Murphy said. "I doubt it. Me and that badge-toter don't get along."

"Why's that?" Clint asked.

"Because he's terrible at his job, but you know . . ." Murphy put his elbow on his desk, and his chin in his hand. ". . . I heard some yelling a little while ago."

"From where?"

"Upstairs," Murphy whispered, and pointed at the ceiling.

"Who would that be, do you think?"

"Well, my neighbor down here is another lawyer, and he's not even in his office, today," Murphy said. "Upstairs you've got Harold Valeski who deals in investments, although I don't know what he's investing in around here."

"And the other?"

"His name's Gregory Davis, and nobody really knows what he does. He just comes in and—" Murphy shrugged, "—sits."

"But does he yell?" Clint asked.

"Not usually," Murphy said, "but I guess something could've ticked him off."

"I guess I'll go up and find out," Clint said. "Thanks for your time."

"Time's all I've got until the circuit judge gets to town," Murphy assured him.

Clint left the office, passed the one that was supposed to belong to A.S. Thatcher, Attorney-at-Law, but was empty at the moment. It occurred to Clint that Rick Hartman would have needed a lawyer in town. He was going to have to find out which one it was, Murphy or Thatcher, and were there others?

He got back to the lobby and went up the stairs to the second floor. He decided to leave the investor for last. He was more curious about the man who didn't seem to do anything but come into his office and sit.

He got to the door that said "Gregory Davis" on it and knocked. He realized this was the office right above the lawyer's office he had just visited.

"Come!" someone shouted.

Clint opened the door and entered. The man was sitting at a desk in the outer office, rather than the inner one. Clint couldn't help but wonder what was in there.

"Can I help you?" the man asked. He was in his early forties, a handsome man, barrel-chested, with black hair and very clear blue eyes.

"Are you Gregory Davis?"

"I am."

"And your business is . . ."

". . . investments."

"What do you invest in?" Clint asked.

"Nothing."

"I don't understand," Clint said. "Then what—"

"You see," Davis said, "I don't invest *my* money, I invest *yours*. That is, if you came in here with money and you were looking to invest it, I would advise you. Understand now?"

"I do," Clint said.

"And do you have money to invest?" Davis asked.

"I do," Clint said, "but that's not why I'm here."

"All right," the man said, calmly, "then suppose you tell me why you *are* here?"

"I'm looking for someone in this building who was just visited by the sheriff."

"Sheriff Erickson?" The man laughed. "I don't think he has two nickels to rub together, let alone invest."

"Well, he may have been here for another reason," Clint said.

"Before we go any further," the man said, "why don't you tell me your name?"

"It's Clint Adams."

"Ah, yes," Davis said, "I heard you were around."

"If the sheriff was here to see you, you're going to hear a lot more of me."

"Now, whoa," the man said, holding his hands out, "I heard you're looking for whoever killed Rick Hartman. Don't look here. I had nothing to do with that."

"Your neighbor downstairs says he heard yelling up here a little while ago," Clint said.

"Now that's odd."

"What is?"

"I heard yelling from downstairs," Davis said. "You're talking about the lawyer under me, right? Andrew Murphy."

"That's right."

"Well, there's your yeller," Davis said. "That man shouts all the time."

"At who?"

"At anybody who happens to be in his way," Davis said. "I guess that could include the sheriff."

For some reason, Clint believed him. He turned, ran from the room and down the stairs. When he got to the attorney's office, the door was unlocked, and he was gone.

Chapter Thirty-Five

"Andrew Murphy?" Otto repeated.

"Yes," Clint said, "A lawyer. Did you ever hear Rick mention him?"

"I can't say I did," Otto said. "Does he say he was Rick's lawyer?"

"We didn't get that far," Clint said. "He got me to leave his office and then disappeared."

"So you think he's involved in Rick's murder?"

"He's got to be," Clint said. "He and Sheriff Erickson had a yelling match this morning. What else could they be arguing about?"

"Have you asked Erickson?"

"Not yet," Clint said, "I wanted to see what I could find out about the man. Have you ever heard Cora mention him?"

"No, never," Otto said, then added, "but ask 'er yourself. Here she comes."

Clint looked over at the steps, as Cora led the three saloon girls down to work.

The girls spread out to work the floor, and Cora came to the bar.

"What are you fellas talkin' about?" she asked.

"Andrew Murphy," Clint said.

"Who?"

"A lawyer in town," Clint said. "Did Rick ever mention him?"

"Murphy," she said again, shaking her head. "No, I never heard the name."

"Did Rick have a lawyer?"

"I think he did, but we didn't discuss it," she said.

"But you were in business with him."

"I worked for him," she said. "I took care of the girls. I wasn't his partner."

"I wonder how many lawyers there are in town," Clint said, looking at Otto.

"I dunno," he said. "I never even heard of this Murphy, fella."

"Well," Clint said, "I've heard of one other lawyer, in the same building." He finished his beer. "I'm going to go back and check."

Good luck," Cora said, as he turned and left the saloon.

***

Clint went back to the building where he'd seen both Davis and Murphy. The other lawyer was A.S.

Thatcher, in room 103. He went to the door and knocked.

"Come in," a woman's voice called.

He entered, found another outer office empty, but this one had a desk.

"In here," the woman's voice said.

He walked to the other office, found a woman sitting at a large desk.

"I'm sorry," he said, "I'm looking for Mr. Thatcher."

The woman smiled, a pleasant smile in a pretty face that had seen forty years or more.

"That would be my father," she said.

"Yes," he said, "Mr. Thatcher, the attorney?"

"No," she said, "Mr. Thatcher is my father, but I'm Thatcher, the attorney."

"A.S. Thatcher?" he said.

"Yes," she said, "Adelaide Sarah Thatcher. You can see why I go by A.S. Can I help you with something?"

"I'm sorry," he said, "I'm confused. I was looking for my friend Rick Hartman's lawyer."

"Yes, that would be me," she said. "Oh wait, are you—you must be Clint Adams, the new owner of the Palace?"

"Yes, I am."

She stood up from behind the desk and came around to shake hands.

Chapter Thirty-Six

"Please," she said, "have a seat and tell me what I can do for you."

He sat and said, "You don't see many female lawyers out here in the West."

"That was what your friend said," she commented. "I think that's why he hired me." She spread her hands. "I'd offer you something, but as you can see, I have nothing."

"How many clients do you have?" he asked. "Just out of curiosity."

"Rick Hartman was my only one. What can I do for you, Mr. Adams?"

"Well," Clint said, "for one thing, you can continue to represent Rick's Palace."

"For money?" she asked.

"Of course, for money," he said. "If Rick trusted you to be his lawyer, I'll do the same."

"If that's the case," she said, "you're on the clock as of now. And thank you."

"What can you tell me about your neighbor?" Clint asked her.

"Murphy? Not much. He's a lawyer, has more clients than I do."

"Like who?"

"Oh, men with money," she said. "Men with an eye toward going places."

"Like the mayor?"

"Oh, no, the mayor has no money," she said, "but Murphy has some members of the Town Council as clients."

"Interesting."

"Why do you ask?"

"I think he had something to do with Rick Hartman's murder."

Her eyebrows went up in surprise.

"I find that hard to believe," she said.

"Why is that?"

"Well . . . he's a lawyer," she reasoned. I'd hate to think an officer of the court is guilty of murder. Or conspiracy to commit murder."

"But do you know him well enough to say he isn't?" Clint asked.

"No, I don't."

"Have you been here all morning?"

"I have."

"He told me you weren't here."

"Why would he do that?" she asked.

"I don't know, but when I went back to his office five minutes later, he was gone."

"He's probably visiting clients."

"Did you hear shouting from his office this morning?" Clint asked.

"Actually, I did."

"That was him and the sheriff."

"Mr. Adams," she said, "since I'm representing you and the Palace, perhaps you should tell me everything you've been up to since you arrived in Mission City."

So he did . . .

***

After she listened intently without interrupting, she said, "Well, you certainly have been busy."

"Yes, I have."

"But tell me," she said, "when you do find the man responsible for Mr. Hartman's murder, are you actually planning to kill him?"

"Yes."

"I think, Mr. Adams," she said, "my fee just went up."

Chapter Thirty-Seven

A.S. Thatcher wasn't all that much help, but at least he had someone representing the interests of Rick's Palace. And on the other hand, she did tell him that Murphy had members of the Town Council as clients. She just couldn't tell him which ones.

"Thank you for your time," he said, standing.

"You'll get my bill," she said. "Shall I send it to the saloon?"

"Yes," he said, "I'll be there for a while."

"Then I look forward to seeing you again."

He left her office, stopping momentarily to confirm that Murphy still wasn't in his.

As he left the building, he felt he was finally getting somewhere. He was certain that Sheriff Erickson and the lawyer, Andrew Murphy, were involved in both the murders of Rick and Abe Ripley. What he didn't know was who was giving the orders. Was it Murphy, or was the lawyer simply the middleman, passing orders to Erickson?

Clint stopped at the Blue Slipper Saloon. He didn't go in but was able to peer over the batwing doors and see the entire room. Murphy was not there. Next, he went to the Bent Tree, saw that Ellie was still behind the bar, so he went in.

"Murphy," she said "yeah, he drinks in here. Quite a few of the men call him Murph. Why are you lookin' for him?"

"I'm sure he's involved with the killings," Clint said, "I just don't know if he's pulling the strings, or somebody's pulling his. Who does he drink with when he's here?"

"Well, you won't like this, but I did see him with Tillman a few times."

"You're wrong," Clint said. "I do like that. Have you ever seen him drinking with Sheriff Erickson?"

She nodded.

"Yeah," she said, "A time or two."

"It's all coming together," Clint said.

"Are you gonna kill the lawyer?" she asked.

"That remains to be seen," Clint said. "I'm still interested in finding out who actually pulled the trigger on Rick Hartman."

"Wouldn't you be more interested in who sent him?" Ellie asked.

"Normally, yes," he answered, "but Rick was shot in the back. I want the man who did that."

"I see," she said. "What if Tillman did it? You already got him."

"Then I'll find out who put him up to it," Clint said.

"Can I ask you a personal question?"

"Sure, if you give me a beer first."

She drew the beer and set it down in front of him.

"Okay," he said, after a sip, "ask away."

"If you don't get to kill whoever shot Rick Hartman," she asked, "will you be disappointed?"

"You're damn right I will."

"Disappointed that you don't get to kill a man?"

"*This* man," he said, then added, "or woman."

"Wait," she said. "If it's a woman, you'll still kill 'er?"

Clint finished his drink and said, "Thanks for the beer," turned and left.

***

After leaving the Bent Tree, Clint went to Rick's Palace. As usual, Rick's was obviously making a profit. All the tables were occupied, and there was no room at the bar. But in the back of the room, Rick's table was empty, so he went there and sat down.

Moments later Melanie, the blonde, appeared.

"Can I get you something, Mr. Adams?"

"I'll take a beer."

"Right away."

She had to dodge many grasping hands on the way to the bar and back, then set his beer down.

"Thanks, Melanie."

"Anytime."

Clint sipped his beer, thought about continuing to search for the lawyer, Murphy, or just going to have supper. While he was trying to make up his mind, he became aware of a path opening up in the crowd of patrons. Suddenly, he saw A.S. Thatcher walking toward his table, still wearing the business clothes she'd worn in her office. They were severe, but did not hide her womanly figure, which was attracting attention.

He stood as she reached him. Once the men in the place knew she was looking for the Gunsmith, they lost interest.

"I thought I might find you here," she said.

"Would you like to have a seat?" he asked.

"I wondered if you had eaten supper, yet," she said. "I was on my way and decided to stop in here and invite you."

"To supper?"

"Yes."

"Since you're my lawyer," he asked, "am I buying you supper, or are you buying me supper?"

"I only thought about eating together and, perhaps, getting better acquainted," she said. "I didn't think about who would be paying."

"Well," he said, "if you pay and we're on the clock, I'd actually be paying, so why don't we just say it'll be on me?"

"So you accept my invitation?"

"I do," he said. He sipped his beer, then put it down and stood up. "Let's go."

***

Since she lived in Mission City, he told her he would rely on her to choose the restaurant.

"Do you like steak?"

"It's my favorite."

"Then I'll take you to my favorite place," she said.

She had brought her buggy to the saloon, so Clint took the reins and she directed him to the Mission Steakhouse, where they were shown to a table too close to the front window.

"I'd like something away from the window, maybe in the back," Clint said.

"Of course, sir," the waiter said.

The restaurant was doing a fine business, most of its tables occupied, but he was able to show them to a table for two in the rear.

"Is this more to your liking, sir?" the waiter asked.

"Yes," Clint said, "thank you."

"Miss Thatcher? The usual?" he asked.

"Yes, Bruce," she said, "for both of us." As the waiter walked away, she looked at Clint. "I hope you don't mind."

"This is your place," he said. "I'm in your hands."

Chapter Thirty-Eight

Clint felt that Thatcher—he decided to think of her that way instead of Adelaide, or A.S.—had some ulterior motive for inviting him to supper but waited for her to get to it.

Meanwhile, he learned that she was from Philadelphia, where she got her law degree, and then decided to come out West to ply her trade. Lately, however, she had been thinking about returning East.

"I don't think the men out here are enlightened enough to accept a female attorney," she said.

"Why don't you try Denver? Or San Francisco, rather than going back?" he asked. "I think you'd be more accepted there."

"That's an idea," she said. "I assume you've been to both those cities."

"I have," Clint said, "as well as Chicago and Kansas City, two other possibilities. I've also been to Philadelphia and New York."

"Did you enjoy going East?" she asked.

"I did," Clint said, "but there usually comes a point where I'm ready to return West." He didn't bother telling her he was born in the East.

After supper the waiter asked if they wanted dessert. They both decided on peach pie and coffee.

"How was your steak?" she asked.

"Just right," he said. "I think I've found where I'm going to eat the rest of the time I'm here."

"Just out of curiosity," she said, "what are your plans after you've . . . found Mr. Hartman's killer and . . . taken care of him?"

"I haven't thought that far ahead."

"Do you think you'd stay here and run the Palace?" she asked.

"Oh, no," he said, "I'll be on my way when it's done. I'll probably leave the Palace in the hands of Cora and Otto. Do you know them?"

"I don't," she said. "As a matter of fact, I've never even been there. Mr. Hartman and I always did our business in my office."

"I see," Clint said. "Well, if I'm going to leave them in charge, and keep you as the attorney, I suppose I should take you over there and introduce you."

"That's actually what this supper was about," she said, finally getting to the point. "I was wondering, if you leave town, would I still have a job."

"Well, that's going to depend," he said.

"On what?"

As the waiter came with dessert, Clint leaned back to allow him to serve and said, "On how good this peach pie is."

***

The pie was excellent, but Clint still had some questions for Thatcher.

"I need to know one thing," he said, "and please don't be offended."

"Go ahead," she said.

"Did you and Rick ever have a more personal relationship?" he asked.

"You want to know if I slept with him?"

"Well, Rick *was* known as a ladies' man."

"My relationship with him was strictly professional, I can assure you."

"So is there a man in your life who might have thought you were having a relationship with Rick?"

"I do not have a husband or a gentleman friend who might have killed Rick Hartman," she said. "Is that what you want to know?"

"That's exactly what I wanted," he confirmed.

"And I'm not offended at all," she said, picking up her coffee cup.

***

After supper Clint settled the bill and they stepped outside the restaurant.

"Can I see you home?" he asked.

"Since we took my buggy here," she reasoned, "if you drove me home, you'd have to find your way back. I could give you my buggy, but I usually drive it to work. So I guess my answer is no, there's no need for you to see me home. In fact, I'll drop you at the saloon before I head home. That makes the most sense."

"I see you've given the matter some thought," he said. "I guess it makes sense for an attorney to also be a very sensible woman."

They got into her buggy, this time with her at the reins, and headed for the Palace.

When they pulled up in front, he asked her, "Would you like to come in now and meet Cora and Otto?"

"I think another time," she said. "I'd prefer to head home before it gets much later."

"Well then," he said, stepping down from the buggy, "thanks for supper."

"We'll talk again soon," she said, "about business."

He touched the brim of his hat, and she snapped her reins to get her horse moving.

Chapter Thirty-Nine

Clint decided to talk with Otto and Cora separately about the possibility that Rick had a woman in hiding. Otto would be easy to discuss it with, but it would take careful wording when talking with Cora.

"You're back," Melanie said, greeting him at the bar. "I didn't see you leave."

"It was on the spur of the moment," Clint said.

"Can I get you anythin'?" she asked.

"I'll just get it from Otto," Clint said. "Thanks, Melanie."

"Sure thing, boss."

She turned and hurried away. Clint stepped to the bar, made room for himself by using his elbows. A couple of men turned to look at him, but apparently recognized him, and moved.

Clint got Otto's attention and waved. The bartender came over with a beer in hand.

"Who was that lady I saw you leave with?" he asked.

"She was Rick's attorney."

"A lady lawyer?" Otto said. "And a fine lookin' one, at that."

"And she's smart," Clint said. "I'm keeping her on to represent the Palace."

"Have you told Cora?"

"Not yet," Clint said. "I wanted to talk to you about something first."

"Hang on," Otto said, "I'll be right back."

Otto moved down the bar, served a couple of customers, and then came back.

"What can I do for ya?"

"Cora was Rick's woman, wasn't she?"

"She was," Otto said, "but you could've asked her that."

"That's not what I want to ask you," Clint said. "Were there any other women? Maybe one who had . . . a husband?"

"You're thinkin' Rick may have been killed by a jealous husband?"

"It's possible," Clint said. "Or a boyfriend."

Otto rubbed his jaw.

"Rick was always busy," Otto said. "He didn't always have time for Cora."

"So you never saw him with another woman?" Clint asked. "Maybe one of the girls who works here?"

"Oh, no," Otto said. "Any of the girls would've loved to be with Rick, but he wouldn't have it."

"Do any of these girls have boyfriends? Husbands?"

"Not that I know of," Otto said. "They all have rooms upstairs and no one ever spends the night with them."

Clint drank his beer while Otto again went to serve someone else. When he came back, he leaned his elbows on the bar.

"Are you gonna ask Cora these questions?"

"I was going to. Why?"

"If there was another woman," Otto said, "I could see her doing somethin' to her, but not to Rick."

"Did Cora and Rick meet when he first came here?"

"Yes."

"Then they couldn't have been in love," Clint said. "I mean . . . in that short time?"

"Maybe not Rick," Otto said, "but I don't see any reason why Cora couldn't have been in love with him."

"Maybe," Clint said, "I should ask her that."

"Maybe," Otto said. "What about the lawyer? Did you ask her if she was having relations with Rick?"

"I did. She said no, their relationship was purely business."

"And did you believe her?"

"I did."

"But she's a lawyer," Otto said. "In my experience, lawyers lie very well."

"That's true," Clint said. "I'll be talking to her again, soon."

"Excuse me," Otto said, "looks like we're gettin' even busier."

"I understand," Clint said. "Go to work."

"I'll bring ya another beer when I get a chance," Otto said.

"That's okay," Clint said. "I'm going to turn in."

He finished the beer he had, set the glass down and walked to the stairs.

"Mr. Adams?"

He turned, saw Melanie.

"Just call me Clint, Melanie."

"All right, Clint," she said. "I was wondering, maybe, later, after I finished work maybe you'd like me to, uh, come to your room?"

"I'm flattered by your offer, Melanie," Clint said, "and I'm probably going to want to talk to you at some point, but I don't think tonight's the time."

"Oh, well, all right," she said, "Just so long as you know I wasn't talkin' about just, uh, talkin'."

"I understand," Clint said, "which is why I said I'm flattered."

"All right," she said. "I better get back to work now."

Clint smiled and went up to his room.

Chapter Forty

By the next morning Clint was feeling frustrated. He had been hoping to have Rick's killer taken care of by now. He decided he was going to have to become even more aggressive with both Sheriff Erickson and the lawyer, Murphy. One of them was going to give him some answers.

Otto had coffee ready when he got downstairs, but Clint declined.

"I'm going to get my answers today," he said. "I don't have time for coffee."

"How do you intend to do that?" Otto asked.

"Erickson or Murphy," Clint said. "I'll beat it out of them, if I have to."

"If you assault the sheriff—"

"He's a poor excuse for a lawman," Clint said. "He'll deserve whatever he gets."

As Clint left the saloon, Otto didn't know who to feel more sorry for, the lawman and lawyer, or Clint himself.

***

Clint went directly to the sheriff's office. Erickson was lucky he wasn't there, for Clint was ready to drag him over his desk.

Next, he went to Andrew Murphy's office, but the door was locked. He kicked it in, found the place empty. He was about to leave the building when he decided to stop in and see Thatcher. She was in her office, smiled as he entered, but frowned when she saw the look on his face.

"What's wrong?"

"I was looking for Murphy."

"Why?"

"I was going to drag him over his desk and make him talk," Clint said. "Have you seen or heard him, this morning?"

"No, nothing," she said. "In fact, I don't think anyone else is in the building."

"Damn it!" Clint hissed. "I have to find them."

"If I can help—" she started.

"You can't," Clint said. "You're better off keeping a safe distance from me. If they know I'm after them, they'll make a try for me."

"Please," she said, "be careful."

"I think I'm past being careful," he said and left.

***

In another part of town, Sheriff Erickson and Andrew Murphy were addressing six other men.

"The last three men we sent after the Gunsmith didn't fare well," Murphy said. "One's dead, one was arrested and the other just ran."

"Then you hired the wrong men to begin with," Justice Tripp said.

"Jus is right," Dave Horace said. "This time you have the right men."

"If we have the right men," Murphy said, "then I want Adams dead by the end of the day."

"Well," Jus Tripp said, "yer payin' us enough."

"Then get to it," Murphy said.

The six gunmen rose and left the room, and the building, which was an abandoned structure on the north end of town.

"You *are* payin' them an awful lot of money," Erickson said.

"That's okay," Murphy said. "They aren't all going to live long enough to collect."

"You think they're gonna get killed?" Erickson asked.

"Some of them will," Murphy said. "Remember, we're dealing with the Gunsmith."

"So we're sendin' them out there to be killed?" Erickson asked.

"Hopefully," Murphy said, "some of them will kill him. Those are the ones I'll be paying. Now, you better stay out of sight until the job's done."

"You mean hide out?"

"That's exactly what I mean," Murphy said. "Hide."

***

Outside the six men huddled together and listened to what Justice had to say.

"I think the best way to do this is to find Adams and just open fire," he explained,

"On the street?" one of them asked.

"On the street, in a saloon, wherever we find 'im," Justice said.

"What if some innocent bystander gets killed?" yet another of the men asked.

"Look," Justice said, "we got the law on our side, don't we?"

"Sheriff Erickson?" Dave Horace said. "He's useless, Jus, you know that."

"Usually," Justice said, "but in this case, he's gonna be very useful."

Chapter Forty-One

Clint took a walk around the main section of town, where he assumed he might find the sheriff, but there was no sign of him. Neither did he see Andrew Murphy, anywhere.

Clint walked to the Palace and stopped outside for a last look at the street. It was probably a safe assumption that Murphy was hiding from him. Possibly even Sheriff Erickson. But there was no point in doing that if there wasn't some plan afoot to deal with him.

He decided not to go inside the Palace but wait outside and see if anyone made a try for him. It was risky. If they sent enough men after him, he might join Rick on boot hill. But if he could grab one alive, he might be able to find Erickson or Murphy.

He went inside the Palace only long enough to grab a chair. As he sat down in plain sight of the street, Otto came out.

"Makin' a target out of yourself?" the bartender asked.

"I need something to happen," Clint said. "This is the best way to make sure it does."

"Do you want some help?" Otto asked. "I can grab my shotgun—"

"You're better off staying inside, Otto," Clint said.

Otto looked around.

"Seems like people are takin' your advice," Otto said. "They must figure somethin's gonna happen with you sittin' out here."

"Good," Clint said, "word will get around. Now you better go inside. And keep Cora and the girls off the street."

"Right."

Otto went back inside and locked the door.

Clint looked up and down the street. As Otto had said, it was empty. His presence in front of the Palace was being interpreted as trouble brewing. He loosened his gun in his holster and kept his eyes alert.

***

"What's he doin'?" Horace said.

"Whataya think?" Justice said. "He's waitin' for us."

"How's he know about us?"

"Not us, specifically," Justice said. "Just some-body."

"Maybe we should let 'im wait," Horace said.

"If we had time, I would," Justice said, "but they want him dead by the end of today."

Justice and Horace backed into the alley they were peering from. The other four men awaited them there.

"Okay," Justice said, "two of you circle around so you can come at him from the other side. Two of you on this side. Horace, you and me are gonna go right at 'im. With any luck, he'll think it's just the two of us."

"Sounds good to me," the man named Lindsey said. "I don't wanna go right at 'im."

"Me and Horace are faster than you four," Justice said. "Makes more sense for it to be us."

"Great," Horace said.

"Let's move," Justice said. "I'm givin' you four ten minutes to get into position."

Justice and Horace moved back to the mouth of the alley while the other four got into position.

"Are you ready for this?" Justice asked Horace.

"I guess so," Horace said.

"Come on, Horace," Justice said. "We live by the gun. Isn't this what we live for?"

"Maybe not for long . . ." Horace said.

***

"What's going on?" Cora asked Otto.

He turned away from the window and looked at her. She was wearing a robe, not yet having dressed for the day.

"Clint's outside," he said.

"Doing what?"

"Just . . . sittin'. Waiting for somebody to try and kill him."

"What?" she said. "And you're just . . . watching?"

"Not only me," Otto said. "The whole town is watchin'."

"Is he crazy?" she asked.

"No," Otto said, "he's tryin' to draw out the people he's after."

"They shot Rick in the back," she said. "What makes him think they won't do the same to him?"

"Well, for one thing," Otto said, "he has his back against the front wall of this place."

"Otto," she said, "you have to help him."

"Don't worry, Cora," he said. "When the shootin' starts, me and my shotgun will be there." He turned to look out the window. "That's why I'm watchin'."

She walked to the opposite side of the front entrance to look out the other window. From there she could see Clint's legs stretched out.

"He seems to be . . . relaxing," she said. "He's an odd man."

Chapter Forty-Two

Clint saw the two men walking up the street until they reached a point across from him. He could tell from the way they wore their guns not who, but what they were.

They stepped into the street and started for him but stopped halfway. Clint drew in his outstretched legs. He kept his eyes on them, but his ears were telling him other things.

"Clint Adams?" one man asked.

"That's me."

"My friend and I are curious—"

"You and your *friends* are being paid," Clint said, cutting him off.

"Friends?" the man asked.

"Yes," Clint said, "there are two more to my left, and two to my right."

"How do you know that?"

"I can hear them."

That seemed to annoy the man, and his companion seemed to become agitated.

"You should know," Clint said, "that as soon as somebody touches a gun, even if they kill me, I'll kill the two of you."

"You mean you'll try."

"Oh, there's no doubt about it," Clint said. "You'll both die."

"Well," the man said, "there's one way to find out."

"Before we do this, what's your name?" Clint asked.

"Justice," the man said, "Justice Tripp."

"Why don't you tell me who hired you, Justice," Clint said, "and then walk away."

"I can't do either one of those things," Justice said. "Sorry."

"Yeah," Clint said, "I'm sorry, too."

Justice went for his gun, and that put everyone and everything into motion.

Clint knew he had him beat, but he had to throw himself sideways, taking the chair down with him, before firing, so that the lead coming from either side went over his head.

He knew his bullet struck Justice in the chest, so he turned his gun on Horace and gifted him with a similar chunk of hot lead.

Then he had to scramble as the other four shooters redirected their aim. Bullets started to come closer, and he dragged himself into the street behind a horse trough.

***

"Otto!" Cora shouted, at the sound of the first shot.

As Clint's bullet hit Horace, the man convulsively pulled the trigger of his gun. The window Cora was standing at shattered, and Otto grabbed her and yanked her down to the floor.

"You have to help him!" she shouted at him.

"I will," he said. "You stay down!"

Otto hurried to the bar, grabbed his shotgun, and was out the door.

***

Clint saw the saloon door open and Otto the bartender appeared in it.

"Otto, get down!"

Otto dropped to the ground just as an array of bullets flew over him. If Clint hadn't yelled, the bartender would have been riddled with lead.

On his back, Otto directed his shotgun to his right and pulled the trigger, sending one barrel on its way. He then rolled over onto his stomach and fired the other barrel. He didn't see if he hit anyone, as he was then rolling into the street. He slammed into Clint and came to a stop behind the same horse trough.

"You should've stayed inside like I told you!" Clint yelled at him.

"Did I hit anybody?" Otto asked.

"I don't know," Clint said, "but I want at least one of them alive."

Otto ejected his spent shells, dug two more from his pocket and loaded them.

"Okay Otto," Clint said, "watch where you're firing that thing."

"How many are there?" Otto asked.

"There are four left, two on each side," Clint said. "And they've taken cover."

Otto's head swiveled both ways before he spoke.

"What about the other two?"

Clint turned to look at the two bodies in the center of the street. Justice Tripp and his partner were still there, and still dead.

"Don't worry about them," Clint said. "Since you're here, you watch the right, I'm going left."

"Do I get a raise after this?" Otto asked.

Clint didn't even give the question some thought.

"Absolutely!"

Chapter Forty-Three

Clint moved to one end of the horse trough and stared down the street. Both shooters had chosen their own doorways to fire from. If he didn't want to keep one alive, he would have simply opened fire. Instead, he wanted to pick at least one of them off, maybe with a leg or shoulder shot, but they were both presenting small targets.

He heard Otto's shotgun let loose with one barrel again. He took the opportunity to break from cover and run to a buckboard someone had left on the street. The two men fired at him.

From behind the buckboard he had a better view of them, which they realized too late. He fired twice, hitting each man in the back of the thigh as they tried to run. They both fell to the ground. Clint then heard Otto's other barrel.

Then silence.

"Otto?"

"I'm fine."

"I got my two," Clint said.

Otto came up alongside him.

"My two got away, but I think I wounded one."

"Let's see who these fellas are," Clint said.

They walked to the two fallen men, both of whom were groaning in pain. Around them people were coming out of their shops to have a look. There was no sign of Sheriff Erickson.

Clint reached the men and used his foot to turn one over onto his back.

"Ahhh," the man cried out, grabbing his thigh.

"Who are you?"

"N-nobody," he said. "Just guns for hire."

"Who hired you?"

"J-Justice."

"No," Clint said, "somebody hired the six of you. Who was it? Who's paying you?"

"Nobody," the other man said, rolling onto his back. "We ain't been paid, yet, and now we won't be."

"No, you won't," Clint said.

Clint heard someone approaching, turned and saw the doctor.

"They're all yours, Doc," he said. "They're no good to me."

The doctor pointed to a few men in the gathering crowd, and they helped him get the wounded men to his office.

"You're lettin' them go?" Otto asked.

"I'll stop by the doc's office a little later," Clint said. "I want them to think they're going to walk away from this."

Otto looked down at himself and said, "I better get cleaned up and open the saloon."

"Thanks for your help, Otto," Clint said.

"Hey," the bartender said, "you promised me a raise."

"And you'll get it."

Together, they went into the saloon, where Cora was waiting with her arms folded.

"You must be crazy!" she scolded Clint, while Otto went to clean up.

"Not crazy," he said. "Frustrated. I thought this would help me find who I was looking for. Now I still have to find Erickson or Murphy and wring it out of them."

"Well, good luck," she said. "Erickson's the sheriff, and where is he? With this much shooting on the street, he should be here. He's obviously in hiding."

"I think it might be time for the mayor to step in and name a new sheriff," Clint said.

"You?" she asked.

"Hell, no, not me," Clint said, "but once he relieves Erickson of the job, I won't be putting my hands on a lawman."

"If you find him," Cora said.

"*When* I find him," Clint corrected.

Suddenly, Cora looked down at herself.

"I have to get dressed, and you should get cleaned up," she said.

"I agree," Clint said. "I'll wash up and then go see the mayor."

***

"You want me to what?" Mayor Pierpont asked.

"Name a new sheriff," Clint said. "I believe Erickson was involved in the killing of Rick Hartman and Abe Ripley."

"Can you prove it?"

"I will," Clint said, "once I find him, and he can't hide behind a badge."

"You do know that sheriff is an elected office, right?" Pierpont asked.

"Hey, you're the mayor," Clint said. "What you say goes."

"Look, I can't just—"

"I'm going to end up killing him, Mr. Mayor," Clint said, "And probably anybody associated with him."

"Who did you have in mind to replace him?" the mayor asked. "You?"

"No, not me," Clint said. "I'm sure you must have some men in town who can do the job."

"Maybe," the mayor said, "but there would have to be some men who want the job."

Chapter Forty-Four

In the end, Clint pretty much had to threaten the mayor into yanking Erickson's badge. By the time he left the mayor's office, the man was no longer sheriff. He also found out that the town had given Erickson a house on the South end of town.

"What do you know about Andrew Murphy?" Clint also asked, before he left.

"Not much," Pierpont said. "He's a lawyer."

"Do you know any of his clients?"

"Now that you mention it," the mayor said, "no."

Clint was determined to find the now ex-sheriff and the lawyer.

He found it was more of a shack than a house. He peered in the windows, didn't see anyone, then forced the front door. The place was both musty and dusty, and it wouldn't have surprised Clint if Erickson slept in the jail instead of there. He looked around but found nothing but dirty clothes.

The mayor didn't know where Murphy lived, and he doubted Thatcher knew, since she didn't seem to know the man all that well.

He left the shack and walked back to town.

***

"Six men!" Murphy snapped. "Six men couldn't do the job?"

"He had help," Erickson said. "Who knew the bartender would come out with a shotgun?"

The two men were once again meeting in the abandoned building.

"And now you're not even the sheriff, anymore," Murphy said.

"What?"

"Yes, Adams got the mayor to pull your badge."

"So who's the sheriff?"

"Pierpont hasn't named anybody yet," Murphy said. "But Adams is out there looking for us, and now we don't even have your badge to hide behind."

"So what-a-we do?"

"I'll have to find out from my client," Murphy said.

"Are you goin' back to your office?" Erickson asked.

"Hell, no!" Murphy said. "And don't go back to your shack, either."

"I never shoulda got involved in all this," Erickson said.

"Hey," Murphy said, "nobody told you to smother Abe Ripley. That was your doing."

"He was fallin' apart!"

"All you had to do was get him drunk enough," Murphy said. "Just stay out of sight until I get some instructions."

"Stay outta sight where?" Erickson asked.

"Right here," Murphy said. "I'll be back."

Murphy left the building, hoping Erickson would obey and stay right where he was. All the lawyer had to do was pass the word that the ex-sheriff was there. Then Adams would find him, kill him, and be satisfied.

***

When Clint returned to the Palace, Otto had opened for business, but the place was pretty empty as it was still early in the day. Besides, the citizenship wasn't sure there wasn't going to be more shooting in the street.

As he entered, Otto waved him over to the bar.

."Somebody just came in and said they knew where Erickson was," the bartender said.

"Just like that?"

Otto shrugged.

"I guess word got out that you're lookin' for him."

"So where's he supposed to be?"

"Some abandoned building on the North end of town," Otto said.

"I'll check it out."

"You want help?" the bartender asked.

"No," Clint said, "you stay here. I'll take care of this myself."

He left the saloon and headed North.

***

Clint found the abandoned building, but didn't go right in. This was either a trap set for him, or Erickson was now being offered up. Either way, he would approach the building carefully.

Instead of using the front door, he circled around to the back. It was a large building, probably once used as a warehouse. Now it was too far outside of where the town had been built up.

He got to the back where there was a large door for loading and a smaller one. He tried the small door, found it unlocked, and went inside.

Chapter Forty-Five

The inside of the building was dim. He hesitated just inside the door to give his eyes time to adjust. When they did, he saw that the place was empty. It had high ceilings but wasn't that well-built. Some light came through the walls.

He was in one large room, but there were doors in the opposite wall. Carefully, he crossed to those doors and tried one. He found it locked. Moving to the next door, he found it unlocked. Slowly, he opened it. It was a smaller room, but just as empty. Then he heard a noise, as if someone was moving around. It sounded like it came from the locked room next door.

He went to the locked door. He knocked, and nobody answered.

"Erickson? I know you're in there. Come on out, let's talk."

He waited, and as he was about to knock again, the door unlocked and then opened inward. Erickson appeared, with his empty hands outstretched.

"Just stand still," Clint ordered, plucking his gun from his holster.

"How'd you find me?" Erickson asked.

"Someone came to the Palace and told us where you were. Who do you think would do that?"

Erickson thought about it for a moment, then said, "That sonofabitch!"

"Murphy?"

Erickson nodded.

"He's the only one who knew I was here."

"I guess he figured I'd kill you and be satisfied," Clint said.

"I didn't kill Hartman," Erickson said.

"What about Ripley?"

Erickson's face reddened and he looked ashamed.

"Yeah, I did that. But I didn't kill your friend."

"Do you know who did?" Clint asked. "Who pulled the trigger? Who gave the order?"

"I don't know any of that," Erickson said. "I was just doin' what I was told."

"By Murphy?"

"Yeah."

"Then maybe he can answer my questions."

"He probably can."

"Where is he?" Clint asked. "Is he coming back here?"

"He should be," Erickson said. "He told me to wait."

"He told you to wait so I could kill you," Clint said. "He's not coming back."

Erickson looked dismayed.

"You're probably right."

"Then where is he now?"

"He went to get his instructions."

"So he's not in charge."

"Only here in town," Erickson said. "He had to go and see his client."

"His client," Clint said. "Probably his only client. And a rich one, at that."

"Yes."

It had to be one of the ranchers Clint had visited.

"Where is he, Erickson?" Clint asked.

"If I tell you, you'll kill me."

"You've got that wrong," Clint said. "If you don't tell I'll kill you."

***

"What are you doing here?" Andrew Murphy's rancher boss demanded.

"I left Erickson behind, and let Adams know where he is."

"Why'd you do that?"

"I figure Adams will kill him, and be satisfied," Murphy said.

"He'll never believe Erickson killed Hartman," the rancher said. "What happened to those six men?"

"Four of them are dead," Murphy said, "two were wounded tryin' to run."

"Where are they?"

"At the doctor's."

"What do they know?"

"Nothing," Murphy said. "They were to kill Adams, and then get paid."

The rancher stared at him.

"Have you talked to the woman about buying that Palace?"

"No," Murphy said. "She's the attorney for the business, and for Adams. He'd have to be gone before she could do anything like selling it."

"If he kills Erickson like you planned and then leaves, that may be enough."

"Maybe."

"You get back to town and find out what happened. Then let me know."

"Right."

"And Murphy."

"Yeah?"

"This is your last chance."

Chapter Forty-Six

Murphy had ridden out of sight of the house when a rider intercepted him.

"Wait!" the lawyer said, putting his hands out. "Don't kill me!"

Clint pointed his gun at the lawyer.

"Are you armed?" he asked.

"Hell, no," Murphy said. "I'm just a lawyer."

"So you didn't shoot Rick Hartman?"

"I did not."

"Do you know who did?" Clint said, "Do you know who pulled the trigger."

"Yes, but you're not going to like it."

"Why not?"

"Because you've already killed him," Murphy said. "Tillman did it."

"On whose orders?"

Murphy didn't answer.

"Never mind," Clint said. "I know what ranch you just came from, which means I know who's giving you your orders."

"What are you going to do?"

"First, we're going back there," Clint said. "Then I'll decide. Turn your horse around."

***

When they got to the ranch house, they both dismounted and tied their horses off. They went to the front door and Clint kicked it in.

"Show me," he said to Murphy.

Murphy took Clint down a hallway to a doorway, and as they entered, Rachel Randolph fired the gun she was holding. The first two bullets struck Murphy and the rest went over Clint's head as he dropped to the floor. When the hammer fell on the empty chambers in the gun, he stood up and pointed his gun at her.

"Go ahead," she said. "Do it."

"What was the point of all this?" he demanded.

"After my husband died, I discovered he didn't have nearly as much money as I thought," she said. "When your friend came to town, I recognized his energy and knew he could build a successful business. I wanted part of it, but he wouldn't sell. So I waited for him to finish building and open, and then figured if I got rid of him, I could buy it for a song. I didn't know you were going to come to town."

Clint looked at Murphy, saw that the man was dead.

"So everybody you used is dead," Clint said. "Murphy, Tillman—"

"Murphy told you about Tillman, did he?" she said. "I told him I wanted Hartman out of the way, and he chose to shoot him in the back."

Clint's rage at having lost Rick was still in him, but now it was intensified by the fact that he didn't get to kill Tillman again, now that he knew he had pulled the trigger. The only one left to kill was Rachel Randolph.

His finger tightened on the trigger.

***

Clint sat behind Rick's desk and signed his name, then pushed the contract over to Cora and Otto.

"We are each going to own thirty-three percent of the Palace," he said. "All you have to do is sign your names."

Cora went first and signed, and then Otto.

"The only demand I have is that Rick's name remains," Clint said.

"Clint," Cora said, "you can be sure this will always be Rick's Palace."

"Agreed," Otto said.

"Then we're partners," Clint said.

Clint stood and shook hands with both of them, and the deal was sealed.

"Do you have to leave today?" Cora asked.

"I'm afraid I've had enough of Mission City," Clint told her.

"Can't say I blame you for that," Otto said.

They all left the office together and walked to the bar. Otto went around and got into position to open, while Cora walked Clint to the door.

"Are you sorry?" she asked him, as they stepped out the door.

"About what?"

"That you brought her in instead of killing her," Cora said.

Clint had dragged Rachel Randolph from her house, put her on Murphy's horse, brought her to town and put her in a cell. He then went to the doctor's office and dragged both injured men to the jail and dumped them in a cell, as well. And then he was done. They were going to be the responsibility of whoever the new sheriff was.

"I can't tell you how close I came to pulling the trigger," Clint said.

"But you didn't because she was a woman?"

"No," Clint said, "I didn't because her gun was empty."

Coming April 27, 2021

THE GUNSMITH
469
The Tall Texan

**For more information
visit:** www.SpeakingVolumes.us

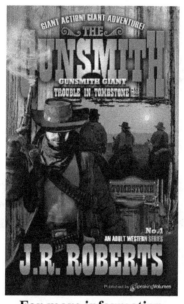

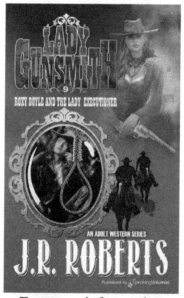

On Sale Now!

Award-Winning Author
Robert J. Randisi (J.R. Roberts)

For more information
visit: www.SpeakingVolumes.us

Sign up for free and bargain books

Join the Speaking Volumes
mailing list

Text

ILOVEBOOKS

to 22828 to get started.